Mars landing revelations

Nicole Barnes

Contents

Chapter 1

"All systems green. Initiating lander separation from mother ship. Separation in two minutes."

The female voice was calm and impersonal while counting down their fate. Well, the AI was only doing its job.

Floyd was a pro. He wasn't nervous. Nervous astronauts soon turned into dead astronauts, and dead astronauts made bad colonists.

The droids had done the groundwork. Alpha station was ready, awaiting their arrival. Their equipment had landed safely; the provisions, the building material, the computers—even PEMAR, the Personnel Mars Rover, was sending signals it had arrived safely and enjoyed robust health.

Goosebumps broke out on his arms and spine. No, he wasn't nervous.

Equipment was one thing, human lives were something entirely different.

"Separation in one minute."

Floyd scanned the control panel one last time. All systems were still green, ready to go.

Ready to eject the landing pod with him, Leelawati, and Bones and send them hurtling toward the red planet, where they would crash-land on its dusty surface.

Crash landings were the safest way to get equipment to the surface. He knew that. Recent missions had confirmed that SHIELD really worked. Its accordion-like, collapsible base acted like the crumple zone of a car and absorbed the energy of a hard impact. Much better than using only parachutes in Mars's thin atmosphere. That was really dangerous, and that's how the first teams of pre-colonists were lost.

Rest in pieces.

SHIELD worked, period. And they would be the first humans to write home about it.

Mars, the final frontier.

"Ten seconds to separation."

Leelawati turned in her seat, her golden visor facing his. Floyd gave the mission's biophysicist a thumbs-up.

Somewhere behind the visor would be her trademark derisory smile, but there was no point in thinking about that now. He had a mission to complete.

"Five."

Bones, the missions engineer and medical expert, checked his safety harness again.

No harness would save them if SHIELD failed.

"Three. Two. One. Separation."

At first, nothing happened, but that was normal. There was always a delay until the impulse reached its destination and did what it was supposed to do.

Like it did now.

The pod shuddered, jerked, and suddenly the figures on the control panel changed. They were moving, accelerating away from the mother ship. It would remain in orbit, recording their descent and possibly the pod's disintegration...

Cut it out, dammit.

"Separation successful."

The theme from Alien burst from the speakers.

"Bones!" Leelawati's voice, transmitted directly into Floyd's right ear, reminded him of the crack of a whip. "Turn that off."

"No sense of humor," grumbled a gravelly bass in his left ear. "We're in space. We shouldn't even hear you scream."

"We're in Mars orbit, not in space," Leelawati said.

Floyd suppressed the urge to roll his eyes. "Cut it out. Both of you. I've got a ship to monitor."

"Yeah, bouncing Mathilda," Bones said. "Oh well, if you insist, man." The eerie music stopped, but its echo seemed caught in Floyd's helmet, ricocheting around and around.

Numbers crawled over the screen. Descent had started.

The inflatable heat shield and decelerator sitting at the front of the pod was another innovation, but that one bothered him less. It had been tried and tested throughout many missions with landers, droids, and the heavens knew what stuff the science team had hurled at the unsuspecting planet's surface. The thing was cool. No bigger than an airline carry-on it expanded to 20 feet and would withstand temperatures of 30.000 Fahrenheit.

The numbers on his screen scrolled faster.

"Going down," Bones said. "First floor, ladies' underwear."

"You're a dinosaur, that's what you are," Leelawati snapped. "Just because you're an Aborigine doesn't mean you can take liberties as you please."

"Yep, fossil and proud of it."

Floyd turned down the transmission to a whisper. If anyone wanted something from him, they could use the override button.

Something rumpled.

"Heat shield deployed," the AI announced in the same flat tone that would have hailed the making of pancakes.

Why was he thinking of pancakes? Was it burning he smelled?

Floyd sniffed.

He did not.

Perhaps he was getting too old for this shit. He never had shown nerves before. But then, he never had landed on Mars.

He itched to grab the controls, but there was nothing he could do. The pod was in autopilot mode. He could only monitor their progress. Intervention and mission override was only for dire emergencies. Which this wasn't, thankfully not. The numbers slowed. The heat shield was indeed up and slowing their descent.

Well, what else did he expect?

This was the Atlantic Alliance's hi-tech, after all. Not only were they pretty good at that sort of stuff, they also went to some bother to ensure their space teams stood a chance of survival. That wasn't always a given with the Pacific Alliance. There, human life came cheap.

And investing into the crews paid off. Mars Mission 1 would be up and running while the PA kept creating more craters with their landing pods.

They too would see the light, but it might take a while.

Hopefully forever.

Someone tugged at this spacesuit and Floyd bit down on a scream. He cranked up the transmission.

"Yeah?"

Bones' golden visor was facing him, and Floyd could swear the whiteness of the man's toothy grin was visible even through the plating.

"I asked how long we have before the fun starts."

Floyd checked. "Any second now."

"Ah." Bones fidgeted with his harness.

The cabin was getting warmer. That too was normal, nothing to worry about. As long as the shield held, they'd be fine. But he'd hated the simulated landings at Red Base. A bit like a teeth-shattering magic mountain fun ride, only without the fun. Bruising was standard, even broken ribs not completely out of the picture.

The AA wasn't all that caring about their crews. As long as they got down without smearing gore all over Mars's frosty surface, all was well.

Any second now.

The numbers rattled over the screen. Final approach.

One hundred meters.

Fifty.

"Brace for impact," the AI announced in the same flat tone.

Floyd braced.

With a rumble that drilled into his teeth, the pod slammed down, only to spring up again, like an oversized jack-in-the-box.

Down, up. Down, up. Rinse and repeat.

Despite the harness, despite the hug-all airbag in the seat, every bone in his body was squeezed by a giant fist that pressed the air from his lungs. His teeth hurt, his brain was pounded into a mash, and a freight train was rumbling through the tiny cabin.

Triple screaming blended into the din, but it was swallowed away.

Then the banging and rocking eased.

The pod shuddered one final time and lay still.

A metallic taste filled Floyd's mouth. He must have bitten his tongue.

"Ow," he said.

"Shit," Leelawaati said.

They had arrived.

Chapter 2

P EMAR's tracks ate up the miles in a teeth-rattling monotony, churning up enough dust for the geeks back on Earth to spot it with their telescopes. For a second, Floyd felt like waving. He didn't give in to the urge, since no one would see him inside this metal breakfast box anyway, and his two companions wouldn't have understood.

Well, Bones with his misdirected sense of humor would laugh at the grim reaper's bony face.

Leelawati wouldn't recognize humor even if it bit off her nose. That was assuming humor made it past her helmet. Since the thing was built to withstand even rocks flying around in a marsquake, it was unlikely.

"How much longer, navigator?" Leelawati asked.

Bitch.

"The man has a name," Bones said mildly. "It's Floyd."

"He's here to transport us to the station. When at the station, his purpose is to ensure functionality of the equipment at all times and to provide mobility services to the scientific crew. That's you and I, Doctor Jones."

"Djalu, my dear. We're going to be in this together for quite a while. Let's take it easy on the formality. Who needs family names, anyway?"

"It's Dr. Kalal, Dr. Jones."

"You're a pain in the back, that's what you are," Bones said.

Floyd tuned them out and focused on his driving. He would provide mobility, all right. If she didn't watch it, she might find herself transported to somewhere rocky and devoid of air sooner than she could say navigator.

Quite a while later, the coordinates had gradually inched up toward their destination. He switched on the external long-range camera, and there it was.

Home sweet home. At least for the next twelve months it would be.

Two domes flanked by squarish, chunky buildings that were connected by an elongated tunnel peeled from the dust. Originally off-white, the dwellings had already taken on a faint rosy tinge.

On Mars, the dust always won.

Black figures moved around the buildings, a bit like artificial guard dogs, only sporting too many edges and angles to be natural.

The droids.

At the edge of the compound sat the oxygenators, large squares with blades rotating in the ever-present wind. Their job was to suck up the carbon dioxide and spit out oxygen.

There was plenty of carbon dioxide to go around, 95% of the planet's blasted atmosphere was filled with it.

To prepare for their arrival, the oxygenators and the field generators had been running non-stop for two years. The machines' combined efforts had created an atmosphere around the dwellings that wasn't exactly healthy, but at least they wouldn't have to wear spacesuits when stepping outside.

Which they would have to do a lot. There were plants to be seeded and grown, the environment to be explored and mapped, the compound to be extended for the next team to join them—yup, they would be busy. With a bit of luck, it would stop Leelawati from mouthing off all the time.

They weren't married, nor would they ever be, so he didn't need yackety-yak on a drip feed. Mona had overdosed him on that.

He wouldn't think of Mona now.

"Target in sight," he said.

"What target?" Leelawati asked.

"Lemme guess, a big, lime-green polar bear, waving the Alliance flag."

Beside himself, Floyd was intrigued. "Why lime-green?"

Bones tapped the side of his helmet. He'd be grinning again. "This is Mars, my friend. The inhabitants are bound to be green."

That didn't deserve a comeback.

"Ten minutes to target," Floyd said in a voice as monotonous as the AI. Yay, he could best the AI any time.

Floyd DeNeville, navigator, Jack-of-all-trades, master minion at your service.

They clanked past a satellite dish the size of a small garden pond, pointing at distant Earth. The thing had arrived in parts and been the first piece of equipment to enjoy the crash landing. Three years the droids had taken to assemble the antenna and get it to work. Yet another piece of technology for him to babysit.

You wanted it that way.

The compound grew with every rotation of the tracks. At least they could stand upright. Half of the training had been spent in gloomy tunnels and the cramped hellholes of the original compound. When too many of the prospective colonists went mouth-frothing mad, the tekkies had returned to the drawing board and threw out something marginally more humane.

Twelve months of Leelawati in a hamster cage. Unthinkable.

He brought PEMAR to a halt.

"We're here. All systems are nominal, which I guess is good."

"You guess or you know?" Leelawati asked, a snappish tone in her already sharp voice.

This time, he couldn't hold back. "Your guess is as good as mine."

"Don't squabble, children," Bones said, for once sounding serious. "We've arrived with only some bruises to show for our efforts. Thanks, Floyd, for getting us here."

"All he had to do—"

"Was to program the trajectory for the pod so the autopilot would take us to PEMAR and not somewhere a lot less conducive to our health. Then he had to calculate the right ground route, which means one that takes us to base camp without running out of battery juice. You give it a rest, lady. You're slowly starting to piss me off something chronic. Believe me, you don't want me pissed off."

"Hah."

But she shut her sniping gob.

Floyd snapped off the safety belt and scrambled from the seat. "I'll go first."

"Why?"

The blessed silence hadn't taken long.

"Because I know how things are supposed to look like. And I'm the one with the environmental scanner."

"Surely, navigator, you don't expect the Pacific Alliance to run interference? All their colonists are dead. And in the unlikely event they sent out another team, which then had to have overtaken us—"

"Unlikely, as you say. But their droids might be running wild. And if someone's managed to change their programming... well, I guess I need not say more."

For once, Leelawati kept quiet. With a bit of luck, that might even last a while.

The door hissed open and Floyd descended the steps, taking care to keep a good grip on the railing. He'd practiced in zero gravity, and this was way better, but it still would take him a while to get adjusted to his new environment where gravity was only one third of Earth's.

Puts a whole new meaning into the expression "a spring in his step."

His weighted soles kept him stable, little puffs of dust rising with each step. A quick scan of the terrain revealed nothing untoward.

Yet an odd sense of dread crawled down his spine.

Something wasn't quite as it was supposed to be.

He held out the scanner and let it travel over the antenna, the dome, the droids.

Nothing.

Then he saw it. One of the large struts that was meant to support the bigger home dome for the next crew was sagging. Not by much, but it was definitely misaligned, riding lower in the ground than the other three, as if the ground below had given way.

His mood plummeted to the planet's frozen magnetic core, where the giant dynamo that eons ago powered Mars's magnetic field lay silent and dead.

Someone would have to fix this shit. Someone meaning him.

Bloody Leelawati would laugh her ass off.

Chapter 3

G ravity was a funny thing. There was less of it here on Mars, one third of Earth's. But despite making it easier for Floyd to lift and lug things, he didn't enjoy what passed for walking on this orange dust bowl of a planet: A loping gait, a bit like running, because he had to lean into it, with a sort of floaty phase in between until he hit the ground again. I took a while to get used to, even for an avid jogger like him.

It got him places, though.

He slowed. It would be stupid to slam into the strut of the future home dome while day-dreaming.

More to the point, he wouldn't hear the end of it. Leelawati excelled at first-class nagging. During the past two weeks, he'd learned to tune her out. No matter what he did or said, she did or knew better. She'd turned into a constant irritant, like the rash on his skin where a seam of his spacesuit rubbed chafed his thighs.

So be it. If it boosted her rocket.

Floyd stopped, fumbled the tablet from the holdall, and pawed at the screen in his gloved hand. After the third attempt—spacesuits weren't really compatible with touchpads, no matter what the techies said—the screen lit up and displayed the latest scan.

There was a cavity under the fourth strut. It hadn't been there when the scientists searched for a suitable site. However, it had been very much there when Floyd surveyed the place for the first time, and it had constantly shown in each and every blasted display, no matter how he calibrated the asshole scanner.

When the powers that be had chosen the site for the Atlantic Alliance's colony, there had been no holes in the ground. Apart from the cavities left behind from the ice-mining, obviously. A colony needed water, the more the merrier.

But those were much closer to the surface. This beast of a hole was about ten meters down. Somehow, its roof had caved in when the struts were inserted into whatever passed for solid ground in this place. A tricky mixture of sand had shifted and the strut with it.

Not good. Not good at all.

"Fix it," Leelawati had said.

As far as he was concerned, he would shove her chubby body into the hole and be done with it. But that wouldn't fix their problem either. One strut was unstable. And if that was the case, all the others were in the wrong place as well. To find another site and move everything across would take ages. They would never be ready for the next stage.

Leelawati knew it. Bones knew it. Floyd knew it.

Shit. How was he supposed to fix the unfixable?

Something about the latest scan caught his eye.

He checked. Now that was bloody impossible. He squinted. Turned the tablet upside down.

It still gave the same reading.

The blasted cavity was no longer ten meters below the surface. Instead, it was just below the surface. Right under his space-booted feet, actually.

Shit.

He couldn't help it. He jumped backward. Only, he was on Mars, and the result was a semi-somersault that slammed him straight into the stricken strut.

Ow.

The life support pack he carried on his back somewhat dulled the blow, but it still wasn't an experience he'd wish to repeat any time soon.

He stood, halfway expecting a sinkhole to open in the ground. It didn't. The wind, a muffled grating in his ears, blew, the dust shimmied around in eddies, and an indifferent sun glowed on the scene.

His lips as dry as the dust, he ran another scan. And another.

Same result.

"Floyd? Base calling." Bones's voice boomed into his eardrum. "How's tricks?"

"This is Floyd. Tricky. Our favorite cavity has risen to the surface."

"Huh?"

"Well, according to my reading, it's not where it used to be. It moved."

"The thing can't move."

"Bones, the thing shouldn't have been there in the first place. I saw the subground scans of the site. No cavities. Then there is one. Then it rises. Either the instruments are totally fucked, or someone is playing tricks on us."

"The AI?"

"Don't blame the AI all the time. Someone ballsed something up, big time, and that someone is human. My money is on the Pacific Alliance."

"Their technology isn't as good as ours. If we can't create holes that move—which I'm sure we can't—they won't be able to either." It's got to be a technical glitch."

"Listen, there's no point in me being out here. There's no point in proceeding until we know what the heck is going on here."

"You wanted to pour plastocrete down the hole to stabilize the strut. Sounds like a good idea to me. Why don't you go ahead."

"What if I pour plastocrete down that hole and it moves somewhere else? Waste of some good plastocrete."

"Ah. Now that would be a bit of a bugger, I agree. Are you sure the thing has moved. I mean it can't—"

"Don't tell me what it can't do. It just does."

"Hey, no worries, mate. I hear you."

Did Bones ever take anything seriously?

"Listen, can't you dig it up?"

"Dig what up? The cavity?"

"Yes. If it's that close to the surface, you shouldn't have any problems. You've got the droid with the plastocrete on stand-by. Just turn on the drill and have yourself a Captain Cook. Just don't actually pour anything before you know what's down there."

That was actually not a bad idea.

"Okay, I'll try my best."

"You do that. Gimme a shout when you're done."

"Don't tell Leela yet."

"Mate, who do you take me for? That woman is missing a few cables in her life support system."

"Okay. Floyd out."

"Good luck. Base out."

Floyd shoved the tablet back into the holdall. He itched take another scan, but where four had shown him a cavity close to the surface, a fifth might well show him one-eyed green aliens baring their teeth, and he really didn't care for that.

He pushed the remote control of the Tekko-Droid.

"Activate."

"Activated."

"Assume pre-programmed position. Aim drillhead at surface. Continue drilling until sub-ground cavity detected. Confirm mission."

"Mission confirmed. Assuming position."

The droid rolled across on its tracks and stopped exactly where the effing cavity was supposedly lurking. The arm with the drillhead rotated and its shiny tip hit the ground. It whirred, the sound distorted by the Mars atmosphere.

"Operation started."

Good. Soon enough they would know if there really was a hole in the ground or not.

Chapter 4

Yup. There was a hole, and it was bloody big as well. The ground radar displayed the cavity in all its glory.

Fortunately, since its roof had been pierced, the mysterious hollow had stayed in situ. They really didn't need mobile underground hazards. Not only were they a bloody menace, but they were scientifically impossible. There was a logical explanation for all this. There had to be.

They only had to find it.

"The unidentified object is exactly circular, with a circumference of 20 meters. That gives us 6.36942675159 for the diameter."

"Just round it up, will you, Dr. Katal?" Floyd said. He'd given up on the first name. There were some people he didn't want to be on a first-name basis with, and sweet little Leela was one of them.

"I never round things up."

Of course not.

"The thingumajig looks like a ball cut in half. Top is there, bottom has been sliced off," Bones said, tapping his finger at the plas-glass screen.

"Don't do that. It leaves stains," Leelawati said.

Bones sighed. But he withdrew his finger.

"The camera scan revealed nothing of further relevance. Apart from an unidentifiable object in the corner." Leelawati's tone conveyed very clearly what she thought of the camera's observational capabilities.

Nothing.

"What's this here?" Floyd would have tapped the screen, but caught himself at the last moment. "There's something on one wall."

"It's unidentifiable as well. This equipment is flawed."

"Looks like we have to ditch the camera and spy with our own little eyes," Bones said.

Floyd sighed. No our. His. The Boy Friday of the mission had just got himself another job.

"Gotcha. I'll suit up."

The Mars atmosphere muffled the boosters' roar, but they worked just fine and deposited Floyd on the sandy floor of the cave, bubble, cavity, or whatever the stupid thing was. From above seeped a diffuse tangerine glow into the place's murky interior. It was late in the day. Normally not the ideal time for explorations, but even Leelawati for once didn't insist on procedures. She was curious, she only didn't want to admit it.

"Floyd to Base. Am on site. Now proceeding to investigate object. Tape and camera activated."

"Base to Floyd. Copied," Bones said.

Protocol observed, Floyd let the beam of his power-torch travel over the smooth walls of the cavity. They lit up in a flare of glitter, which caused the self-adjustable visor of his helmet to enter shading mode, leaving him standing in a black sinkhole.

"Oh, screw this."

It took a moment for his eyes to adjust, but eventually Floyd pointed the torch at the floor and pressed his gloved fingers against the wall. Smooth, not quite like glass, but definitely not rock.

He pointed his scanner at the wall. Readings flickered over the screen.

"Igneous rock detected."

That was a big fat help.

"Which igneous rock?"

"Correlation Obsidian 95 percent. Mica minerals four percent."

Okay, that was possible. Obsidian was basically volcanic glass formed when lava cooled rapidly with minimal crystal growth. Mars had plenty of volcanos, and a huge one was just around the corner. The minerals might be responsible for the flare, though the flare had been rather on the bright side.

But lava bubbles, glittery or not, don't move. He switched off the little voice at the back of his brain. It wasn't telling him anything new.

Having dimmed his power-torch, Floyd turned around and lumbered for the other end of the cavity where the first unknown object lay on the ground.

Now, that was odd.

He was right here, quite close to the damn thing—and he still couldn't work out what he was seeing.

He blinked.

Ah, the dang visor. He raised his hands and pushed the button that deactivated the shading mode.

The chamber was suddenly a lot lighter. He looked down.

A human skeleton lay at his feet.

Floyd couldn't help it. He jumped back.

Of course, this being Mars, he sort of floated, knotted his legs in the process and landed on his butt with a thump. A little cloud of dust rose, floated, and quietly settled again.

"Base to Floyd, what are you doing?"

"This isn't possible." The voice in his ear sounded hoarse, alien, totally unlike his.

"Navigator DeNeville, please adhere to protocol," another voice drilled into his head.

Oh gawd, there was a human skeleton in the chamber and the woman gave him protocol.

His gaze slipped back to the bones, brown and stained they reminded him of twigs. He wasn't the biggest expert on human remains, but the broad pelvis made him think his unwelcome find might have been female.

Perhaps, she too didn't adhere to protocol.

He sniggered.

You're hysterical. Cool it, man.

There was a human skeleton that couldn't be there on the floor of a cavity that moved.

"Navigator DeNeville?"

He breathed in and out. Twice. He felt a bit better. Not much, though.

"Floyd to Base. There's a female skeleton in the cave. At least I think it's female."

Silence roared in his ear.

"Base to Floyd. Repeat that for me."

"Floyd to Base. Confirmed. We have what I think is a female skeleton in our cavity. Which seems to be made of volcanic material, but it's a bit weird."

"Base to Navigator DeNeville. Observation of first object acknowledged. What about the other one? The unidentified phenomenon on the wall."

Leelawati sounded as cool as one of her baby cucumbers she was growing in the new greenhouse.

"I'll check." Sod the protocol.

He turned his back on the remains that shouldn't...couldn't be there, and stepped up to the curving side of the cave.

He squinted.

No, he wasn't imagining things.

There was a writing on the wall. Four words. Or letters. Or glyphs. Or something. The problem was, he couldn't read any of it.

"Floyd to Base. I'll show you what I found." He raised the camera and pointed it at the nonsensical scribbles in front of his helmet.

"What's that?" Bones asked. In the background, Leelawati gave him aggro over protocol.

"Language is my best guess. Just don't ask me which one."

Something flashed.

No, not something. The words flashed, shimmied and shivered. Then, they melted and rearranged themselves into a different shape.

There were still four...whatevers in front of him. But they weren't the same thing he'd observed a few instants ago.

"Did you catch that?"

The answer was a while in coming.

"Yes," Bones said. "Floyd, get the heck out of there. This isn't normal."

"You're not telling me anything new."

"Base to Floyd. Evacuate chamber." Leelawati's voice, was tight, urgent, concerned for once.

He didn't need another invitation. Floyd fired the boosters and rose at the darkening skies. As he ascended, the ray of his torch slid over the sad muddle of bones on the floor. They, at least, hadn't moved.

Chapter 5

"They've changed again." Leela squinted at the viewer and shook her head. She pinched the bridge of her nose and sagged in her chair.

This bullshit with the four words on the wall shimmying into something else had been going on the whole day.

"Let me guess, another variation on the 'squiggly scribble that makes no sense' theme?" Bones asked.

"Spot on."

The enigma of the twitchy letters brought out the human side in the woman. Last evening, when he returned to the home dome, she'd even called Floyd by his given name and not his function.

Wonders never ceased.

He stared at the domed ceiling of the science room and sucked on the tube that contained his dinner. It was bland but nourishing, like the rest of their provisions, until they harvested their first crop.

"If I think about it, I could swear the first set of words I saw down there morphed into something that reminded me of Sumerian pictographs," Floyd said.

Two faces turned at him. Two sets of eyes widened.

Only one person spoke.

"You're an expert in ancient scripts?" Leela asked.

"Not an expert, no. Before I ended up in engineering, I studied a variety of subjects, archeology among others."

Bones and Leela looked at each other.

"But why would there be Sumerian writing on the wall?" Leela asked.

"Perhaps it's biblical," Bones suggested. "Mene Mene Tekel Upharsin. Bible. Book of Daniel, Chapter Five, I believe. Maybe we've been found wanting. Or we're being warned off the planet. Can't see the Persians invading, though."

"Huh?" Leela said. She swished about on her tablet. "Oh, I see."

"Yup, King Belshazzar and his merry men."

"He was Babylonian," Floyd said. "The Sumerians ruled the roost a bit earlier than that," Floyd said. "Plus, I'm really not sure it was Sumerian, though it looked like it."

"If someone wanted us off the planet, they could have blown up the base before we arrived. There's no need for these eccentricities." She sounded as if the moving cavity, the bones, and the spooky writing were a personal offense.

"Hah." Leela pointed at the viewer displaying the wall of the cave with the annoying words. The little camera Floyd had lowered into the hole diligently did its job, even if the image appeared rather grainy.

It made no odds; the writing on the wall was as illegible as it had been from the start.

"They've changed."

"Already? That was quick." Floyd stepped up and examined the image in the viewer. Sure enough, yet another set of symbols had appeared.

Realization whacked him over the head. He pointed at the screen. "Hieroglyphs. They're hieroglyphs."

Leela pushed his hand aside. "Don't touch the screen. I told you before. You're leaving fingerprints."

"Copy them. Quick, before they vanish again."

"There's no need to hurry. We have them on tape, you know?"

"For heaven's sake, I want to know what this says."

"Can you read hieroglyphic?"

Floyd had a hard time not to roll his eyes. "No, but the computer can decipher the text."

"On it." Bones swiveled around in his chair. "Activate main computer."

"Activated," an impersonal female voice said.

"Analyze script currently in viewer. Provide translation, if possible."

"Analyzing."

"If it's gone—" Leela said.

"Then the computer analyzes the tape, just as you said. Are they gone?"

"They're still there," Floyd said.

"Translation available," the computer said.

Floyd's stomach knotted with anticipation. He bent over Bones' wide shoulders and stared at the screen.

The translation stared back. "Meet me at dawn."

For a moment, an eerie quiet filled the room. Other than the soft hum of the air generator   and a gentle creak of Bones' chair, nothing disturbed the shocked silence.

Then everyone spoke at once.

"What the fuck?" Bones said.

"This is illogical. And scientifically impossible," Leela said.

"Meet who? And where?" Floyd said.

Once again, the room was silent.

"Good question," Bones said eventually. "Shootout in OK Corral?"

"It's the Pacific Alliance. They're toying with us. Gotta be," Floyd said.

"How?" Leela asked. "They haven't even arrived yet, and while they might mess with our computers, they cannot actually manipulate our environment."

The woman had a nasty tongue, but a good head on her narrow shoulders.

"Okay, so it can't be them," Floyd said. "But someone is doing something. First, we have a cavity where there was none before. It's deep underground. Until it isn't. Then, I go in, and not only do we have a sub-ground anomaly where there shouldn't be one, but we also have a female skeleton lying around where it doesn't belong. To top it all, we have a bloody mobile inscription our trusty machine identifies to be an invitation for a date."

"About sums it up." Bones nodded.

"Even computers can be wrong," Leela suggested. "We'll send this back to mission control. Let them lose sleep over the riddle."

"Nice try. I don't think we're going to wriggle out of this so easily," Bones said.

Floyd stared at the hieroglyphs. They hadn't shifted. But something about the cave was different, and it wasn't the fading daylight.

Then he saw it.

This time, the skeleton had disappeared.

His breath rasping at the inside of his ears, Floyd boosted from the bottom of the cave. As theories went, the idea of the camera being faulty, wasn't a bad one. Unfortunately, the thing had been functioning just fine. Skelly was truly gone, and the hieroglyphs on the wall remained stubbornly static.

As if someone was watching their every move and once they'd deciphered the script it no longer mattered.

An icy finger of fear tapped at Floyd's neck.

"Floyd to base. The camera is unfortunately not faulty. We're minus a skeleton."

"Base to Floyd, understood. Dr. Kalal here thinks the bones might have been a projection, not really there."

"They were there. I saw them with my eyes. 3D, full color, the works."

"Did you touch them?"

"No, but I stood real close. I'm not blind, you know? I'm coming back. Floyd out."

He stood at the rim of the cavity and squinted into the ubiquitous dust. He had hoped—dreaded was perhaps a better word—to find tire or track marks. Anything that suggested the Alliance was around playing silly games.

But when he arrived, the ever-shifting sands were pristine, and the only footsteps he could see were the ones he made yesterday. Most of them had been blown over, but in the lee of the rocks, some marks had been protected from the endless wind.

What was going on here?

He wouldn't solve the mystery by standing around. Floyd turned and headed for the base, using the fresh set of footprints left behind from his outward trip as a trail marker.

Footprints.

He stopped.

This was impossible. Not only scientifically, but completely and utterly impossible. It couldn't be. This shit couldn't be happening.

There was a second set of footprints close to his.

Chapter 6

The orange haze that announced another evening on Mars threw lengthening shadows on the uneven ground. Riddled with rocks in all shapes, colors, and sizes, the place was dryer than the desert back on earth. Floyd wouldn't have been surprised if a camel rounded the cliffs to his right and eyed him with disdain.

In this place, anything was possible.

His gaze found the ground and the footsteps that couldn't be there.

Impossible like those bloody things.

He squinted into the setting sun. There were his prints in the dust, clearly recognizable by the ridges on the soles.

And next to his tracks was another pair, smaller and look-ing—odd.

He stepped up and regarded the prints on the ground. There was a pointy bit at the front, and a round depression at the back.

What sort of shoe would leave such a mark behind? He would have scratched his head, but the helmet was in the way. Then it came to him.

High-heels.

"Who the fuck would wear high-heels on Mars?" His voice sounded odd. This bloody planet screwed with everything, even his voice.

Leela, even if she were a high-heel person—which she wasn't, on Earth she'd worn sneakers all the time—wouldn't run around with them out here. For one thing, it was too blasted cold. And the ground too rocky. And.

High-heels on Mars simply didn't compute.

Well, nothing did, recently.

Did the skeleton don high-heels and tottered away, just to spite them?

Floyd called himself to order. There was a suspicious track next to his, which meant an intruder had been sneaking around. No matter what Leela or Mission Control back on Earth insisted, his money was on the Pacific Alliance having gotten here before them and now creating chaos to keep them occupied until more troops arrived.

Yes, that was it. Whatever had happened before had been super-odd, but the high heels were over the top. With that, these idiots had betrayed themselves.

"Cut yourselves in the foot with that one, guys," he said to himself.

That didn't stop him from digging out the camera and taking some nice, sharp shots of the heel-prints. Otherwise, no one would believe him. Heck, he hardly believed this himself. His job done, he packed the camera, grunted, and plodded back to his temporary home.

He was very close, the dome, furred with ocher dust, rising before him, when realization whacked him over the head.

The fake footprints were going all the way. Once in a while they were blown over, just like his own tracks, but they doggedly returned, the sharp bits pointing north like a compass back on Earth. On this planet, with its messed-up magnetic field, compasses were useless. But whoever made these prints didn't need one. They had his tracks to guide them.

A sensation akin to a bucket of ice water washing down his spine took his breath away.

His tracks. Guiding whoever was out there straight to the dome.

But surely, they'd known about the dome, had noticed their arrival? They didn't need his footsteps to do...what?

"Floyd to Base. All Roger with you?"

No response.

Shit. He'd known that. How could he have known that. Sixth sense or what? He was developing a darned sixth sense, like a hare chased by an invisible lion.

This planet was a total-screw up.

He scanned his environment. Nothing moved, not even his shadow.

"Floyd to Base. Please respond."

Nope.

Floyd sped up, jumped, floated, landed and bounced again, covering as much ground as possible in the shortest possible time-frame.

ETA three minutes and counting.

And the heel-prints went all the way to the square cubicle containing the airlock, until they vanished behind the gray reinforced plas-steel...the door.

It had been uniform gray when he left. Now, there was an orange splotch on it, close to the handle.

He came to a panting halt.

Not a splotch. The orange imprint of a human hand.

These two idiots had let in an intruder.

Floyd had never been faster through the airlock.

Close outer lock door. Pass through safety channel and open second door. Close that. Activate the environment scan.

A soft pearly light washed over the chamber's interior.

The dusty orange heel-prints on the floor flared like a warning beacon.

Yup, they'd done it. Let whatever, whoever was assing around into the compound.

"Air safe to breathe," said the usual could-not-be-assed-less artificial voice.

Floyd unscrewed his helmet and clomped for the inner door. He was supposed to de-suit before entering the compound, but there was no time for this.

He took his gloves off, but his fingers hat gone into full fumble mode.

"Remove spacesuit before entering the compound," said the same idiotic, prissy voice.

"Shut up," he yelled.

"Code incorrect," the keypad chirped.

He entered the code again.

"Code incorrect. Self-defense mode activates on third wrong attempt."

What the...

Take a deep breath. Relax. You know the code. You just have to enter it.

One by one, he tapped the numbers. The keypad clicked and a green light flared.

"Code correct," the pad chirped.

With a rumble of panels, the inner door opened.

"You'd better remove your spacesuit before entering the compound," said the same voice...Hang on, that wasn't the same voice.

That was Leela's voice. She was standing in the corridor, sucking on a yellow tube, and regarding him with hooded eyes.

"You never know what's out there." She winked at him.

"Where's the visitor?" He shrugged out of his life-support pack.

"What visitor?" Leela asked.

"There's a set of footprints headed for the base. I followed them. When I saw the handprint on the panel outside, I got the heebie-jeebies, believe me. I thought you'd all been slaughtered in your bunks."

She trilled a laugh that sounded completely unlike anything she'd ever uttered before. Whatever was in that tube, he wanted some of it. Like now.

"Nah, we're fine. We were analyzing the hieroglyphs once more, and sent more pretty pictures back home. Mission Control thinks we're making the stuff up, you know. Can't blame them really. First we find hieroglyphs, then we mislay a skeleton."

Floyd slipped out of the suit and stored it.

"I contacted you and got no response."

"Oops, sorry. Shouldn't have happened. I'll have a word with Bones, he was your contact. Anyway, I'm not sure what you mean by visitor. There's no one here but us."

She blinked her lashes at him.

"Look." He pointed at the heel prints on the floor.

Unfortunately, there were none. The tracks had disappeared.

Chapter 7

ones pressed buttons on the robo-medic, and the cuff around Floyd's upper arm deflated with a hiss. Frown lines on Bones's usually cheerful dark face showed something was wrong, but then Floyd had known that already. Middling nausea churning in his stomach, he asked, "What is it?"

"As far as I'm concerned, nothing. our vitals are fine, even if the blood pressure is too high." Bones pulled the stethoscope from his ears and let it dangle on his broad chest. "But other than that, there's nothing to write home about. That's what worries me."

"Why are you worried about there being nothing to worry about?"

"Because you're obviously having hallucinations."

"We all have them, right? We might have imagined those bones in the cavity."

"We have recordings of them. We know they were there. The tracks don't show on your camera. There's just nothing, nada."

"They were there! As were the handprints on the panels."

"Sure, sure," Bones said soothingly.

"I'm not nuts."

"I don't think you're nuts. I just think you need to take it easier for a couple of days. You've been running around like a blue-arsed fly, and that's no good for anyone."

"Have some OJ," Leela said. A yellow tube appeared in Floyd's peripheral vision, and he snatched it.

"What I need is a large beer."

"We haven't got that," Leela said. "It's against protocol." She pursed her mouth and examined the cupboards in the broom cabinet that passed for a surgery as if they hid contraband alcohol.

Well, there was some, but that was for disinfecting things.

"Someone should change the protocol, then." Bones shut down the robo-medic and rolled it back into the compartment where the thing lived. "Once in a while, a glass of a decent red for medicinal purposes can work wonders."

Floyd slumped in his seat and massaged his temples. The tracks had been there; he knew it.

Did he really? Somehow, the events of the last couple of hours melted and blurred into a puddle of doubt.

Through the open door that connected the surgery with the work-space pinged an alert.

"Incoming message from Mission Control."

As one, the prep-team sprang up and entered the work-space.

The communication screen flared and displayed the upside-down triangle of the Atlantic Association in yellow on bile-green.

Fortunately, the psychedelic logo was immediately replaced by the stubbled face of a sour-looking man in his fifties.

"Mission control to Mars base. Do you copy?"

Leela took her seat and flipped the lever that opened the comms channel. "Mars base to Mission Control. We copy."

"It's about your skeleton. The one you mislaid."

A wave of red-hot anger stabbed into Floyd's head, and it started throbbing like a faulty rocket. "We didn't..."

"Communication protocol!" Leela shot him a glance that could have frozen acid, so he shut up.

She smiled at the screen. "Continue, Dr. Paulsen."

The man scowled from the screen. "I can't say I was happy with your find, but I thought it might have been the remains from one of the, eh...failed landing attempts. We lost an awful lot of people there."

"Impossible. No spacesuit," Bones said. "And not only was the skeleton articulated, with all bones unbroken, the thing was also laid out as if someone was sleeping. No one who went through the earlier landing attempts would have been in a shape to lay themselves to rest. Not without a spacesuit, anyway."

"I know that," Dr. Paulsen bellowed, and banged on something hard—hopefully a table and not a control panel—outside their field of view.

Since no rockets launched and the klaxon remained silent, he must have hit a piece of furniture.

"You should have taken a sample when you could. Then we wouldn't have this problem now."

"The sample wouldn't be with you yet," Leela said.

Paulsen banged on the furniture again. "That's beside the point. You didn't, and now you lost that skeleton."

"We didn't lose it," she said. "It vanished."

"Skeletons don't vanish."

"This one did," Floyd said.

Leela rolled her eyes. "Sorry, Dr. Paulsen. He's right, though. It was there all right. Until it wasn't. This is not why you contacted us, correct?"

Paulsen ran his spidery fingers through his thinning hair. "No. That skeleton..."

"What about it?" Bones asked.

Leela raised her arms and let them drop again. "Why do I even bother. Make yourselves right at home, will you?"

Bones grinned. "We will."

"Oh, shut up."

Floyd was sorely tempted to remind her about the protocol, but decided against it. It wouldn't get him anywhere, and it wasn't worth the hassle.

"It's not homo sapiens," Dr. Paulsen said, with an expression on his face as if he'd swallowed a glass full of vinegar.

For a moment, a hush fell over the room.

"Come again?" Leela asked.

"I said, the skeleton is not human."

"You mean...an alien?" Floyd asked. The throb in his head increased. If his blood pressure was bad before, it was going south in a hurry.

"Oops," Bones said.

Paulsen snarled. "I said nothing of the sort. I told you it's not homo sapiens. Nothing to do with aliens. There are no aliens, at least not in this solar system."

"You sure?" Bones asked.

"Yes, for fuck's sake," Dr. Paulsen bellowed. This time, he banged the table twice. Something heavy crashed to the floor.

Leela shifted in her seat. "I'm not sure I understand you. The skeleton is not human, but it's not an alien either?"

"Of course, it's human," Paulsen snapped. "Just not homo sapiens."

The room fell as silent as a small space jam-packed with machinery could ever be.

"Um," Floyd said. "If it's not a modern human, then what is it?"

"Neanderthal," Paulsen said. "Female."

So, his guess had been right. "Those bones looked pretty old."

"The last Neanderthal man...human...whatever died ca 40 .000 years ago."

That was pretty old.

"If I had a sample, I would have half a chance to date the blasted thing," Paulsen said, with a whine in his voice.

"We don't have it, so forget that," Bones said.

"Why would someone dump a Neanderthal skeleton on Mars?" Leela asked.

"To make our lives even more difficult?" Floyd suggested. "I'm telling you. It's the Pacific Alliance. They're here somewhere, and they're running rings around us."

"Stop it," Paulsen said. "Find that skeleton. That's an order. Until I actually get to see the thing, I don't know what to believe anymore. And concerning the Pacificos—they're about to launch, but they haven't—and I repeat—they haven't arrived yet. You're on your own for quite a while. So, continue to prepare the base for colonization, and find that skeleton. I expect an update in 24 hours. Mission Base out."

The image vanished and was replaced by the bilious logo.

Floyd, Leela, and Bones looked at each other.

"Shit," they chorused.

Chapter 8

There was no friggin' point in running further perimeter searches for the missing skeleton. Not when the site was riddled with rocks, blasted by sand, and surrounded by miles and miles of nothingness, where even a the planet's biggest shit pile of bones could vanish forever.

Floyd groaned and buried his head in his hands.

This wouldn't do. He straightened, and faced his companions, whose expressions were as bleak as his must be.

"Everything we've been experiencing is scientifically impossible," Leela said. She'd been saying it before in the last hour. Several times.

"Yeah, unfortunately something or someone here doesn't seem to give two hoots about science," Floyd said.

"That statement is flawed," Leela said. "You're assuming there's an intelligent entity behind these odd happenings. Paulsen just told us we're on our own. Which we knew beforehand. So, there's no someone or something around to give hoots."

"Paulsen is an ass," Bones said.

"Tell me something I don't know," Leela said with a sigh.

"So, what do we do?" Floyd asked. "I've been around the blasted compound twice in the last few hours. So has Bones. So have you. No skeleton. We don't even know where to look. The remains could be under a rock, in a hole, anywhere and nowhere. There's only one thing we can do."

8k MILESTONE HERE

"Such as?" Bones asked.

"We have a dawn appointment, remember?"

"You can't be serious," Leela said.

"I am. We've been wasting our time going after the bones."

"Let's waste them following up on the words, is what you suggest? Mh,why not," Bones said. "It's not like we got much else to do, eh?"

"Nope. I'm only suggesting a change of tactics."

"He's not wrong," Leela said. "That's one approach we haven't tried yet. It would be logical to do so. As irrational as it appears. Eh..." She frowned, apparently lost among the twisted loops of gray matter.

It had been a long day for all of them.

"Fine, why not?" Bones said. "Trouble is, where are we supposed to meet the bus? There's a lot of space around." He waved his arm and swept the procedure manual from the shelf.

"The cavity," Leela and Floyd said simultaneously.

"Hm. Put like that, it makes sense. Question is, who do we send? Floyd baby here shouldn't have been running around like a groundhog on his great day. I really don't like his vital signs."

"I'm fine."

"You're blood pressure is way too high, and that's despite the medication. You need rest and sleep."

"If you think I'm going to snooze while you two go out there and play footsie with the aliens, you've got one coming."

"There are no—"

"Yes, Dr. Kalal," Floyd said. "I get it. No aliens. Maybe it isn't aliens, fine. I don't care. I simply want to know what this shit is all about, and then I want it sorted, so we can continue doing our job. Which is, as Paulsen pointed out so kindly, all about setting up our colony."

"Who wants to live on effing Mars?" Bones asked.

"We do," Floyd said.

"Not forever."

"Thank the non-existing deities for that," Floyd said.

"Bones...Dr. Jones and I will go. You stay here and watch our backs."

He could do that. She sure had a nice ass. Shame really, it was hidden by the space-suit. Even worse it came with such a prickly personality. Having said that, recently she hadn't been too bad.

Wonders never ceased, and he was acting the grunting Neanderthal. Tut, tut, so not politically correct.

In his mind, he could do what he wanted. No one around to tell him off. What were the other two idiots saying?

"...make sure to keep the camcorder running," Bones said. "The last thing we want is something happens and we don't have evidence."

"I wasn't born yesterday." Leela's fingers slid over the touch-board, entering their proposed plan of action.

More ass covering going on, but like the spacesuit, it was necessary.

"You suit up and keep PEMAR in standby mode ." Bones pointed at Floyd. "If anything goes awry, you can gallop to the rescue."

"My blood pressure won't like that."

"Agreed, but hopefully you won't have to actually do any-thing."

Floyd wasn't sure what he wanted. One part of him craved to be in on the action. The other part, bone-tired and freaked out, craved only one thing.

Sleep.

Well, with a bit of luck they would get the regulation six-hours in before the brown stuff hit the air-supply system.

To Floyd's ultimate amazement he did get his regulation shut-eye and some, and a good, deep one it was well. It was nice not to be walking like a zombie, powered by stress, caffeine shots, and suppressed panic bubbling away in the recesses of his mind. With a bit of sleep and a shower under his belt, even this godforsaken world was a much better place. The shelter in its gray uniformity almost looked like a home. Even the artificial scent in the air was bearable.

He sniffed. What was it today? Ah, pine.

Better than yesterday's lemon, for sure. That had reminded him of toilet cleaner.

He held his vitality bracelet against the scanner. It beeped and flashed yellow. Not brilliant, but a lot better than yesterday's piddly two hours.

"Morning," Bones said. He lurched into the control room, wearing his protective underwear in sexy mummy-wrappings beige and holding two mugs of insta-caf, one of which he held out to Floyd.

"Why aren't you suited up?"

"Change of plan. Leela drove around the terrain with the hover cat and had a quick Captain Cook. She's back now, getting PEMAR ready. Spotted nothing out of the ordinary. We'll then walk over together, and see what's what."

Leela was getting the transport ready? That was a first.

Bones emptied his mug. 'I'll suit up while you get kitted out. Gimme a shout, when you're on."

"Will do. And good luck."

"Yeah, we need some of that."

The door hissed shut behind him.

Floyd took a while set up the auto controls that would keep the shelter online while he was in the airlock. The last thing they needed was getting locked out or something. He'd never hear the end of that. He then entered the airlock, which was unsurprisingly empty. Leela and Bones waiting outside.

"Base to Kalal and Jones, do you copy?"

"Copied," two voices chorused.

"Okay, I'm in the airlock. Just have to suit up. Ten minutes to start of mission."

"Copied," the two voices dutifully chorused.

Mission Dawn Patrol was under way.

Chapter 9

Spending time in an airlock was possibly the most soul-destroying waste of time imaginable. The calls to the field team at regular intervals provided little entertainment; they were terse, strictly protocol, and yielded no surprises. Bones and Leela were on their way; then they were in position. So far, they had observed nothing and sunrise was only fifteen minutes away.

No surprises were good in a way, but the roar of silence in the airlock did nothing for his inner ants, swarming his suit.

First Floyd counted bolts. Then, he counted icons on the touch-board. Once he ran out of icons, his gaze fell on PEMAR. He'd better check the thing was in working order. Leela was no technician. She might have bollixed something up.

"Bones to Base. Do you copy?" the communicator squawked.

Floyd extricated himself from the back of their transport and shuffled across.

"Bones to Base?"

Yeah, yeah, try running in a suit.

"Base to Bones. Copied."

"Okay, it's sunrise minus ten. Still nothing, apart from a nice peachy glow on the horizon. We're doing fine. Anything your end?"

Floyd gave the instruments a quick once-over. The perimeter screen displaying the tiny white figures of Leela and Bones was steady, the image crystal-clear. He then turned, scanning the inside of the airlock.

"Nah. All systems green."

"Long may it stay that way. Gimme a holler if you notice anything. Bones out."

This comms hadn't strictly been necessary, and only because Floyd knew Bones well did the tiny quiver in the man's voice even register.

Bones was shit-scared. So would he be, if he were standing in a Martian dawn, awaiting the unknown.

"Base to Bones. Roger and good luck. Base out."

Why was there a quiver in his own voice?

One of the two tiny white figures waved. The other, despite the distance, managed to convey a sense of disgruntlement.

All quiet on the Western front.

He squeezed his space-suited butt onto the support and glued his gaze to the screen. Top right, time ticked by all too slowly in large blue numerals that faded into the grayish-blue haze of the Martian morning.

He shouldn't have drunk the insta-caf. It churned in his stomach like an acid washer.

D minus one. Dawn was almost over.

Mesmerized, he scanned the screen for any movement other than the sun now spreading an opaque glow over the sky. The glow turned brighter and suddenly there was a glitter of light.

The sun was rising.

A wave of relief, tiredness, and frustration washed over Floyd and he sagged in his seat. Despite the suit, its hard surface dug into the small of his back.

No one had been there for the meet and greet. Well, what did they expect?

"Bones to Base. Do you copy?"

"Base to Bones. Copied."

"Well, I guess that was a bit of a washout, eh? No green Martians to say hello? No Pacificos. Nada. Just nothing."

"Maybe they're fashionably late?"

"Huh. You don't believe that yourself."

"Not really, no. Come back, this is pointless. Paulsen will have to accept that the skeleton's gone. And we have better things to do than arse around all the time."

"Truer words were never spoken. We're returning to base. Leela wants to check the oxygen generators first, so ETA will be around seven. Bones out."

"Base to Bones. Copied."

With a sigh, Floyd set the comms unit to standby and slipped off his seat.

He swung around.

His stomach plummeted to the floor of the airlock.

The door to the living space stood open.

He'd closed it. He knew he'd closed the damn thing. Not only that, when he last checked everything in the airlock had been fine. Including the damn door. He would have noticed had it stood open.

This wasn't possible. This simply wasn't possible.

Leela would ride his scrawny ass if she found out.

With a snarl, Floyd activated the life support-functions of his suit.

Helmet—check.

Air-supply pack—check.

Comms functions—check.

With a careful shuffle, he headed for their living space, his heartbeat filling his chest, his head. His whole body was thrumming with totally inappropriate panic as he put first one foot, then the other, across the threshold.

Everything looked just as it should. There was the plastex table, the two mugs of insta-caf still standing on the surface.

There was the tiny galley and the two doors leading to the work-space and the dorm corridor. There was the big porthole that gave them a full view of the perimeter, where two small white figures were still clambering about. That they didn't hurry told him, all was well outside.

Just as things seemed to be here.

But that door shouldn't have been open.

An oversight? Had he simply not noticed.

Rubbish. The door had been shut.

"Why are you wearing this clunky thing? Isn't this your living area where you should relax?" The voice came from behind him, from the airlock.

Something colder than a Martian night slithered down his spine.

The airlock had been empty. Even PMAR had been empty. He'd checked.

He'd checked everything, dammit.

There was movement in his peripheral vision. Someone walked in from the airlock and passed him with slow, measured steps.

The smell of moist soil, of rushing rivers and meadows filled with blooms and bees filled his nose.

Then she was past.

She, yes. Had to be, though it was hard to tell with the complex layers of tawny hide and small pieces of fur that covered her body. She was short, but no shorter than Leela, solid of built, and she had long cinnamon blonde hair that cascaded over her shoulders. Beads and feathers were woven into the glistening locks, and everything shimmied and fluttered as she walked.

In a fluid movement, she swung around.

Floyd took a step back.

The woman's eyes were a bright, piercing blue that shone from under a dominant brow ridge. Her nose was rather bulbous, but it suited the strong contours of her wide, heart-shaped face that radiated a beauty born from strength and competence. Little horn ornaments and feathers dangled from her ears.

His gaze slipped down. She wore a pair of red high heels. He looked up again.

The generous mouth stretched into a smile.

"Greetings, Plainbrain. Finally, we meet."

"Who...who are you?"

The smile lit up her entire face and he could have sworn something among all those furs twinkled and flashed.

"Call me El. My real name you might find rather unpronounceable."

Synapses in Floyd's numbed brain clicked and switched. He'd seen her likeness before. In a museum on Earth when he'd been a child.

"But...you're...you're a Neanderthal."

Chapter 10

T he Neanderthal woman shook with laughter and settled herself on the torture device that served as a sofa.

"A funny name you've given us. But we've done the same, so I guess it's allright. But, seriously, get out of this clunky thing. You don't need it, you know?"

Who are you? What are you doing here, and a whole barrage of related questions slipped through Floyd's mind, only to disappear into a black void.

His gaze slipped to the feet of the apparition. Well, she had to be that. Couldn't be anything else. An apparition born from drugs and too much stress.

"Why are you wearing high heels?"

She wriggled her feet, turning the pointy tops inward. "Hot, aren't they?"

"Not with the outfit you're wearing."

"You think so?"

"Yes."

"That's a shame, for I quite like it that way."

Another thought popped from the limbo that had taken a firm grip on his mind. "Why do you speak AA standard lingo?"

"I'm not. You only think I am."

"What?"

She flapped a lazy hand, the beads around her wrist clicking and clacking. "I talk the way I always do, but I've twisted the language part in the thing you call your brain, so you can understand what I'm saying. It took me a moment to get that sorted. I wasn't quite sure what language you're using these days."

"Took you...the glyphs on the cave wall."

She clapped. "Yes, I'm so glad we finally connected. We've been out of touch for ten thousands of years. Once I knew we had an understanding, I could check you out."

"Check us out?" Duh, now he sounded like a broken record. But his brain wasn't capable of more.

"Well, I needed to know who I was dealing with. So, I went across."

Did she? He'd seen the footprints. But no one else seemed to have done so.

"You're not real. You're a hallucination."

The Neanderthal woman—the apparition who called herself El looked hurt. "That's rather rude of you, you know? We're talking, so how can I not be there?"

"We're talking only in my head. I'm imagining things."

"You're not imagining me." El pressed the palms of her hands togeether and the insta-caf dispenser sprang into life with a steaming hiss.

"How did you do that?"

"Isn't it considered polite among your people to offer your guests a drink? We always invite visitors to the fire."

"The stuff isn't very good. And we don't invite imagined visitors for coffee."

The non-existing visitor smiled and sipped her insta-caf.

Floyd pressed his hands to his ears and pinched hi eyes shut. "Lalalala. You're not there. It's the pills. I'm hallucinating."

When there was no response, he slowly opened one eye.

Was she gone?

Nope. El was sitting on the settee, furs, high heels and all, a mug of insta-caf in her hand. "Since you didn't offer, I haven't prepared one for you."

Floyd's legs trembled. Needing to sit down in a hurry, he lurched to the closest seat.

"Please, go away."

"No, not when I finally got hold of you."

Floyd groaned. "But what do you want?"

She smiled, her strong white teeth gleaming. "Ah, I thought you'd never ask." She placed the mug on the table and steepled her strong fingers. "We knew it was only a question of time until you lot would appear in the dream."

"What?"

"You're not very eloquent, are you? Dream. This." She waved at the rusty landscape outside. Bones and Leela's white-suited figures had vanished, most likely on their way back to base. What would happen if they came in and found him talking to the wall?

What if he wasn't talking to the wall?

"Whose dream? Mine?"

"My people's, of course. Your lot has got little enough imagination. Always did."

"Oho, now you're being unfair."

"If you're referring to the literature, art, and music your people have created, my flat-faced little friend, then you should know this is owed to the genes my ancestors so kindly shared with yours."

"Bollocks."

"How would you know?"

Good question. He didn't. He didn't have an artistic bone in his body.

"Do you now want to know why I'm here or not?"

Floyd sighed. He must have hidden creative talents. The construct created by his mind was disturbingly independent. "Go ahead."

She placed the mug on the table. "You're right, this isn't good. Your people aren't only unimaginative by design, you also lack an essential sense."

"Such as?"

"Such as the dreaming."

"We do dream."

"Yes. Apart from insects and fish, all animals do. But you can't do what we do. Bridge the gap in your dreams is what I'm talking about."

"Gap? You're making this up as you go along, right?" What the heck had been in the pills Bones gave him?

El tugged at the ornaments dangling from her left ear. "You're as dense as soapstone. No, with our dreams we can make things happen. Things that aren't real. Things that are what you lot call impossible. How else do you think I got hold of these shoes?" She waggled her feet. "How else do you think I can walk around in a place that doesn't even have an atmosphere? Or make caves move, eh? Tell me that, little man."

Carefully, Floyd rose and removed his helmet. Then he fetched himself a synth-coke. It tasted just as bad as the insta-caf, but it contained more caffeine. It was high time he woke up, and somehow it wasn't happening.

In the meantime, he might as well ask more questions. "What about the bones we found?" He downed half a glass of synth-coke.

"Oh, those are mine, don't you worry. I didn't trust you not to do something silly with them, like sending them back to the cradle in a probe or however you call that. That's why I pulled them back into the dream."

Floyd spat out his coke. "You did what?"

El rolled her eyes, the blue of an unpolluted sky. He knew how that had looked, since his grandma had taken photos.

"Look what you've done. You ruined your nice floor."

They both regarded the standard-gray floor. "It's not nice," Floyd said.

"Mh. You might have a point on that one. But otherwise, I was wrong. There's something denser than soapstone and it's sitting opposite me. You don't believe me, do you? You still think it's your mind conjuring me up, correct?"

"Uh..."

"Yes, you do. I can see it. I guess I'll have to show you. Otherwise, you'll never get it. And it's important that you do."

"Uh, why?"

"As much as I hate to say it, there's something we need from you guys."

With that, she pressed her hands together.

The environment flickered, lurched, and then vanished altogether.

Chapter 11

Seagulls were the first thing Floyd heard. Their hoarse shrieks really were unmistakable. Seagulls on Mars? Well, the planet was full of surprises. So why not seagulls? Carefully, Floyd unglued one eye.

A flock of the white and gray scavengers were circling over him. Not liking the look in their beady eyes, he sat.

"Shoo. Eff off."

Not much effing-off happened, but at least the avian bastards didn't come any closer. They kept shrieking, but over the bloody racket Floyd could now hear another sound, the boom-boom of a pretty heavy surf. Tangy air laced with ozone found his sensation-starved nostrils. After so many months of living in a processed environment, all this raw nature was pure, joyful overkill.

It didn't take the cockle lying close to his foot, nor the sand clinging to one cheek to tell him he was on a seashore.

There were no seashores on Mars.

Once there were.

Something cold that wasn't wet sand oozed down his spine.

But the sand wasn't orange. And the sky was clear and blue, dotted with the type of puffy clouds that spoke of good weather.

Corrosion. Mars had been rusting away for millennia. Before, it might have looked quite different.

He should have paid better attention to the history files. But he was the navigator cum maintenance worker of the mission, not a bloody librarian.

With a groan, he stood.

And found himself covered in furry hides that covered his shoulders and back. Another crudely tanned hide, this one without the pelt, had been wrapped around his midriff, and dangled to his knees.

He made another discovery. The air was bloody cold.

Not the I'll-freeze-you-to death-in-five-seconds-flat sort of night-time temperatures that existed on Mars, but cold enough. The draft now swirling under hides that unerringly found bits of Floyd not covered by the fur was reminiscent of an arctic outbreak. Unpleasant, but by no means lethal.

Seriously unpleasant.

Damn it, this place was an icebox.

Whatever else this place was. Or whenever it was.

He walked up and down and stomped his bare feet on the sand. His breath came out on puffs of white, and the blasted sand frosted his toes.

But moving sent the blood coursing through his veins, which helped at least a bit with the chill, allowing him to take stock of his surroundings.

He seemed to be in some sort of half-moon bay, cradled by rough rocks that glistened with water. On all sides, steep cliffs rose. They appeared to be reasonably stable, not some sandstone crap. If need be, he could scale them, he was sure of that. A lot of his astronaut fitness training had contained serious hiking and rock-climbing.

The sunlight of what had to be a cloudless morning outlined the cliffs in sharp relief. Some parts of the rock face hid shadows deeper than he would have thought possible.

Caves, perhaps?

Caves were trouble. Recent past had proven how much trouble they were.

At least those holes in the rock face weren't underground. One had to be grateful for small mercies.

Floyd slapped his forehead. Why was he thinking such rubbish? Why were his thoughts skedaddling all over the place like a bunch of upset ants? This would get him exactly nowhere.

There had been this woman, El. The apparition in red heels. She who moved the cave around. She who put the writing on the cave's wall. Somehow, she got into the camp. She claimed Mars was a dream, or something like that. And she wanted something from him. For that, she had to show him something.

Most likely, this was it.

Whatever it was.

"Okay, I get it. You can make me fall asleep and dream funny stuff. Consider me wowed. Can I now return to Mars?"

The sea boomed on, the seagulls shrieked, and somewhere in his chest, his heart bonged away, rather fast.

Other than that and the rushing of the wind, there wasn't much noise.

There certainly was no response.

The base camp on Mars had been a bit of a shite place, but at least it was what he signed up for. He'd expected processed food, sterile air, and cramped lodgings.

He'd even expected danger. Astronauts lived for danger.

He never expected standing at a seashore wearing a crude collection of hides and furs that did little for his body temperature.

"Shit," Floyd said. "Hey, I expect an answer."

Boom, hiss went the surf on the pebbles. The seagulls shrieked, and it sounded like laughter.

He put his hands to his mouth and hollered, "Hello, El. This is getting old."

"Help," someone shouted.

Floyd froze. Not because he was cold, which he was, but because this wasn't the response he'd expected. In all fairness, he'd expected no response. His Neanderthal tormentor seemed to be the kind of person...apparition to tease him a lot longer.

She certainly didn't strike him as someone who'd shout for help.

"Who's there?" he hollered.

"Who are you?"

"I asked first."

"What sort of attitude is that?" The voice, female as far as he could work out, sounded vaguely familiar.

"Do you now want help or not?"

"Uh. Well, I guess I do. What else was I supposed to shout? I needed to announce my presence."

"You could have sung a song, for example."

"I can't sing. Can you?"

"No."

"See?" That sounded distinctly smug and even more familiar. But the voice wasn't El's. It was too sharp, clipped—heavens.

"Leela? Eh, Dr. Kalal?"

"Navigator Floyd?"

"No chance of navigating anything in this outfit."

There was a short, embarrassed silence. "Uh, are you also so...so scantily clad?"

"Furs?"

"Yes. What's this supposed to mean?"

"You're asking me?"

"Who else would I ask when Bones isn't here?"

"He isn't? Are you sure?"

"Very. I combed the whole shitty beach, and he definitely isn't there. Where are you?"

"Do you see some cliffs and rocks and stuff?"

"Yes, right in front of me."

"Okay, that's where I am. Let me see if I can get out of here."

"That would be appreciated." She sounded just as lonely and lost as he felt, and suddenly the urge to be close to another human being, another real person, even if it was Leela became overwhelming.

"Just a mo. I might have to do some climbing."

"Be careful. These cliffs look nasty."

Leela worried about him? That was a first. He suppressed the urge to gloat about his manly pectorals—there was no point, was there?—and scanned the cliffs for a navigable path. Soon he was up where he wanted to be, traversing along a narrow ledge that led to a dip in the cliffs. He peeped over the barrier down at a much larger bit of beach, its far end lost in some sort of opaque mist that could hide a lot or nothing.

Sure enough, there she was. Leela, bitch queen of Camp Mars, the bane of his life—and someone he was mighty glad to see.

Her dark hair, cropped short for the mission, was standing on ends, and she was huddling miserably in a motley collection of furs. There weren't enough of them around to hide the fact she wasn't wearing even the skimpiest fur bikini.

Somehow, the hides and pelts El had worn looked a lot more stylish. But then El hadn't been carrying a spear. The one in Leela's pudgy hands looked distinctly business-like.

Leela looked up and waved.

"Yoo-hoo. Be down with you pronto." He was, too.

"Hey," Leela said, a smile lighting up her austere face. She had pretty eyes, though. Sort of chocolate-brown.

"Hey," he said. "You okay?"

"Guess so. You?"

"Mh. Apart from the idiotic getup, I guess I'm doing all right."

Leela snorted. "Don't mention the furs. What happened? One moment I'm walking back to the camp with Bones...Dr. Jones...oh, to hell with it. The next, there's this beefy broad wearing a pair of fuck-me pumps and grinning like a maniac."

"El."

"Huh?"

"Her name is El. Or so she told me."

"Oh-kay. She said she needs you to understand something, but she believes you'll"—she quoted bunny ears in the chill air—"do better with a companion."

"Well, thanks a bunch."

"Wasn't me who said that."

"I didn't mean you."

Leela shivered, poked the spear into the sand, and pulled her furs closer to her body. "What is this place? Apart from freezing. And what the heck is going on here?"

"I seriously have no clue. But I intend to find out. You with me?"

"Do I have a choice?"

That sounded a lot more like the Leela he knew. Funnily enough, it made him feel better.

Much better.

Chapter 12

B efore any explorations could happen, Floyd and Leela had to sort out minor details like food and shelter. Water had been ticked off already: a small stream trickled down the cliffs, forming a crystal-clear pool at its bottom. Whether that was just a nifty ruse devised by nasty microbes lurking in the rippling fluid was anybody's guess. In any case, they had little choice.

Leela was the one with the spear, so she'd have a go at the fish, of which there seemed to be tons, splashing around in the shallow water of the beach. The driftwood stacked at the far end would make a great bonfire.

If they could light it.

If they couldn't, it was sushi time. There certainly was enough fresh seaweed to spice things up.

Floyd's job was to climb up and explore the caves. It didn't look like it was going to rain—in fact, if there was to be precipitation, it would most likely arrive as snow or sleet. Alone the thought of what nighttime temperatures would look like and what they would do to his body propelled Floyd up the cliff in no time.

Yup, there were caves. They weren't high, they weren't spacious, but they would do nicely as shelter—uh, oh.

Perhaps not.

Floyd took a cautious step closer to the blackened fire ring at the back of what was effectively a generous overhang.

Someone had had the same great idea. And that someone had been there first.

His gaze fell on a collection of crude stone bowls and something that looked like a deflated balloon made of hide.

He lifted it.

Wondered if it would hold water.

"El? Did you leave this for us?"

No response.

Behind the fire-ring lay something furry. He stepped closer. Pelts in all shapes and sizes, stacked up as orderly as the irregular shapes would allow.

"Someone's house-proud, eh?"

Still no response.

A heap of firewood caught his eye. As long as the owners of all this seaside real estate wouldn't show up, they should be snug for the night.

"Better and better," he said to himself.

A draft swirled around his ankles, and he bent down. The firewood had been piled up next to a man-sized hole in the rock. He bent, crawled in, and banged his head.

Not so man-sized after all, the bloody hole.

"Shit."

Careful not to scrape his exposed hide on the protruding stone, Floyd kept crawling and emerged at the top end of what reminded him of a rock slide spilling onto some sort of plateau. Grassland wherever he looked. To the left, the right, and all the way to the horizon a sea of yellowish-green grass undulated in the ever-present wind. Above, the seagulls dipped and dived. Something that looked suspiciously like a rook or a raven—he'd never been able to tell the two apart—was sitting on a boulder, giving him the evil eye.

"El?"

The bird cawed and flew off.

Maybe not.

"We're not on Mars anymore," said a female voice behind him.

It took all of Floyd's tattered self-control not to shriek like a little old lady. Though little old ladies these days were more likely to get out their shotgun, and pepper your guts with buckshot.

He swung around. Leela stood at the exit of the crawl tunnel, shielding her eyes with her hands. Her furs were wet at the bottom, and she smelled of fish.

"Catch anything?"

"Enough to invite guests. Me big hunter." She grinned and banged a fist on her chest. The furs dangling over her chest parted, revealing a rather nice, firm pair of knockers.

Blasted space suits. They gave the word unisex a whole new meaning.

This was so much better.

It also was much colder.

"I'd prefer to stay among ourselves tonight, if you don't mind. What do you mean, we're not on Mars anymore?"

"I recognize these cliffs. Well, I recognize the reconstruction they made at the museum."

"Reconstruction of what?"

"Neanderthal cliff dwellings. La Cotte de St. Brelade."

"Where's that when it's at home? Lemme guess. France?"

"Jersey. The Channel Islands. Neanderthals lived here for over two hundred thousand years until they went extinct."

"Might be their little pad I found."

"I think so, yes," Leela said. "Makes me wonder where they are."

"Gone on vacation? I can only hope so. I really wouldn't like to run into them. El was already built like a linebacker. They might not be keen on guests, especially not those of our ilk."

Leela shrugged. "We cross that galaxy when we get to it. Right now, I'm hungry. I hope you've been in the boy scouts, for I haven't. Someone's got to light a fire."

"You wouldn't be, not when...ehem." Floyd forced his gaze away from her chest area.

"Me girl, not boy. I get it." Her grin was decidedly saucy.

"Eh, yes. Anyway, I can probably get a fire going. The question is whether we should announce our presence."

"We're here. Sooner or later, they're going to find us. Let's light our fire and grill some fish. If need be, it can serve as a peace offering. Come on." She went down on all fours and wriggled back through the crawl space.

A stirring in Floyd's nether regions told him how much a certain organ in his nether regions liked the sight of Leela's deliciously ample behind.

A lot.

Want.

"Can't have it."

The body part in question didn't agree.

Now, this was seriously unprofessional behavior. He was an astronaut, Leela his mission commander and colleague. There was no reason a brief trip back to the Ice Age should make him forget all his manners. Absolutely none.

If push came to shove, he'd keep some ice water handy. There was certainly plenty of that around.

His stomach growled. Now, that was an urge he was more than willing to serve.

Floyd got on his knees and crawled back into the cave.

Much later, the fire spitting embers into the black mouth of the cave, the sky a canopy of stars, Floyd and Leela sat covered in the pelts the cave owners kindly had left behind and stared into the flames. Their bellies were full, they were reasonably warm—especially if they shared a pelt, and the day's adrenaline was fading into a drowsy contentedness.

"What is El trying to achieve with this, I wonder," Floyd said.

"What did she tell you?"

"She said she needed to show me something, so I would understand. Or words to that effect."

"Mh."

"I still don't know who or what she is. At first, I thought I was hallucinating. But if you've seen her as well..."

"I have. So does Bones. He threatened to shoot her."

"Oh, Bones. He'll be alone now. Stranded on Mars. Poor guy."

"We might yet return. That's assuming we're really here."

"Huh? Where else would we be?"

Leela raised her upper body on one arm and faced him. "On Mars? This could be a dream."

"We can't both have the same dream."

"How do I know you're real? I might be imagining you."

"Ah. I'm imagining you. Explains a lot." Floyd grinned.

"Don't be ridiculous." Leela reached over and pinched his cheek.

A sharp pain knifed into Floyd's soft flesh. "Ow. You nuts or what?"

"See? I'm real."

"You didn't have to do that." He sat as well. The fur slipped down his back and he pulled it back up, but not before a cold draft had slithered up his spine.

"Perhaps not. But it was fun."

The woman had a funny notion of fun.

Once again, the cave fell silent, the sound of the surf being the only noise—not quite.

What was that? Somewhere in the distance wavered a thin, high note, like an ethereal call from another world.

"Did you hear that?"

"Yes. I'm trying to ignore it. Might be a dream."

They listened.

The note was still there. A quiet lament, the tune rose and dipped in sync with the surf. And now there was the sound of distant—thunder? Avalanche? Stampede?

The cold draft returned. "Shit. If that's a dream, it's pretty real."

"The whole experience is pretty real, don't you think?"

"Unfortunately, yes."

With a sigh, Leela rose. "Then we'd better have ourselves a look-see."

Chapter 13

F loyd poked at the fire with a gnarly branch. Embers spat in all directions. Acrid smoke billowed into his nostrils. He sneezed. "Not now."

"What do you mean 'not now'?" Leela's posture radiated impatience.

Short of stamping a foot, she had it down pat.

"Means I'm not climbing down a cliff in the dark. Even if I don't break my shins, I might run into a pack of saber-tooth tigers. And then what?"

Leela plopped back on the pile of furs. "You think they might hang around here?"

"I haven't the foggiest. But I'm not going on safari in the dark to find out. Don't forget, we've neither got protective gear"—he pointed at the furs draped around their respective bodies—"nor weapons."

Leela waved her spear. "Got that."

"Yes. One. Which we need for fishing. Well, I guess once we've we've been eaten, we don't need to worry about food anymore."

"That's gross." But she didn't get up. Instead, she wrinkled her nose. She looked cute when she did that. Her large, dark eyes stared into the star-speckled sky outside the shelter.

Woosh. Something pink flared, and faded away again. The rumbling and the distant singing or whatever it was, gained in volume.

"Uh," Leela said. "You saw that?"

"Yes. And I keep hearing things."

"Saber-tooth tigers wouldn't be so noisy, I guess."

"Woolly mammoth? Or maybe it's Sid, the sloth causing avalanches. Or his mates, having a party."

Leela slapped his thigh. "Don't be ridiculous." But she was grinning. "Okay, so we stay here and do nothing."

Floyd held out the fur to her. "You got it. I don't know where you grew up, but my home-sweet-home was in Edingow's underbelly. If you learn one thing, it's not to go where you'd better not be."

"You don't sound like a Scot."

"No." A world lived in that answer, but he wouldn't share it. At least not now.

Leela cleared her throat. "I wonder if El wanted us out there."

"If she did, she could have dumped us in the plain. Which she didn't. So there. That's assuming we're really not hallucinating."

"We're not."

"Wanna bet?"

"I never bet."

The tromping and singing peaked in a shrill screech and pink washed over the sky, the pink of a fiery dawn.

But the leaden tiredness in Floyd's bones told him dawn was hours away. And he wouldn't get much sleep either, not with this racket going on. Not to forget that, despite the warmth of the fire, it was bloody freezing. He knew it. The temperature knew it. The moment the fire went out, they'd have nothing but the furs to keep themselves warm.

Well, that and their bodies.

Despite the fishy whiff of Leela's furs, the thought had merit.

He shifted in his seat.

It would be too bloody cold for that as well.

"I wonder what the woman wants," Leela asked. "There's got to be a point to this craziness."

"Yes, she wants me to understand something. Why me? I never understand anything."

Leela giggled. "You're not that bad."

"Thanks. That's kind coming from you. I thought you didn't like me."

Leela reached for her spear and weighed it in her hand. "That's not true. In fact..."

"What?"

"I liked you quite a lot."

"Huh. Didn't show for sure. Navigator this and Navigator that. Procedures, blah, blah, blah."

She giggled, a silvery tone quite at odds with the prickly personality she had projected. "Oh, jolly good. So that worked."

"What worked?"

"Nothing."

Pink lightning tore at the sky and there was another ear-splitting screech, followed by a deep rumble.

Then it was silent.

Totally silent. No rumble, no singing, no nothing.

Just silence.

"Looks like we've missed the bus on this one," Leela said.

"We'd never have made it there. Which confirms my theory about El."

"You have one?" Leela batted her lashes. They were long and silky, and it was high time he got his inner grunt under control.

"Assuming this is for real, then she's sent us on a time-travel spin. Back to Earth as well. That's pretty nifty, I dare say."

"It's scientifically impossible. Time-travel doesn't work."

"Scientifically it doesn't, you're right."

"Which tells you what?"

Floyd huddled into his fur. Since she'd gotten up, Leela had kept her distance. What was good for his libido did nothing for his comfort.

Their hab back on Mars might have been bland, it might have been sterile. But at least he had been warm everywhere, unlike here, where his front was roasting and his back got assaulted by the clammy chill hanging around the rock.

Quit bitching. It won't get you anywhere.

Sometimes, his inner voice could be a right pain in the ass.

"It tells me we might be dealing with magic."

At first, Leela remained quiet. Then she huffed under her breath. "That's...wild."

"Got any better suggestions? Go right ahead, I'm listening."

"It's been scientifically proven that magic doesn't exist."

"Yeah, like that would work so well."

"Floyd, seriously—"

"I am being serious. What I don't get is why she didn't take Bones for the trip. He's totally into this stuff."

"He is? I thought he's a double doctor."

"He's that as well. Doesn't stop him from believing in things that go bang in the night."

They both strained their ears and listened. But other than the sound of the surf and the wind, the night remained eerily quiet.

"But if he believes in that sort of crap, and assuming you're right and there is something paranormal involved, then why not take him?"

"He wouldn't have needed convincing."

"And that's important because..."

"Search me. For some odd reason, it behooved El to send the two of us on this trip."

"Where she then dumped us in a sea cave on Jersey."

"Not dumped. We have water, shelter, and food. If we'd been dumped out on that plain, we might not have survived the night."

"Because of whatever went on there. Aliens?"

"Because of the cold."

"Ah. Okay. Makes me feel a lot better about myself." Leela wrapped her fur around her and slipped closer to him. "Hey, El," she hollered. "Floyd thinks you're a magician. Do we score?"

Floyd wasn't surprised when the night didn't respond.

"Didn't work," Leela stated the obvious.

"Nope."

"There's something bothering me about that woman."

"Only one thing? Personally, I found the heels a bit much. Didn't go with the fur."

Leela elbowed him in the side.

"Ow."

"What about the skeleton we found? Where is it?"

Floyd heaved a deep breath. That question had been lurking in the back of his mind for quite a while. So far, he'd managed to keep it down.

Bloody Leela and her fishing skills.

"My best guess is we met it."

"Yup, that's what I thought. It's her. Some sort of illusion, perhaps."

"The question here being what is the illusion—the woman we saw or the bones? And the cave. And stuff."

"She can't be both dead and alive."

"Scientifically, no. But we just agreed this has nothing to do with science."

"We agreed? I must have missed that one."

Floyd rolled his eyes, which was a total waste of time, since Leela wasn't even looking at him.

"I still don't get it. What is it she wants you to understand?"

"Something to do with those phenomena we experienced earlier?"

"Mh. Okay. Suggested plan of action?"

"We sleep. Once the sun is up, we have a look, and see if there's something to be found."

"Fine with me. We better keep a watch, though."

"You reckon?"

"Saber-tooth tigers, you remember? Failing that, I wouldn't like to be ambushed by the owners of this fine real estate." Leela patted the furs she was sitting on. "I'll take the first watch."

"Shouldn't I—"

"You're ill, remember?"

With all that shit going on, Floyd had plain forgotten his heart troubles. "Actually—"

"Can you throw a spear? Don't worry, if a flint stone sales-person calls, I'll wake you up."

Jeez, the woman who never joked had just cracked a joke.

"Wake me up in four hours, okay."

Leela tossed him a funny look. "I'll wake you up when I get too tired. We're not wearing watches, remember?"

There was that.

Floyd had hardly placed his head on a rolled-up bundle of fur, when sleep sucked him into a dark, black void.

Chapter 14

An ocean surged through Floyd's dreams, something which wasn't only totally ridiculous, but downright impossible. There were no oceans on Mars, not anymore. There also shouldn't be this odd reek of woodsmoke, fish, moldy walls and—what? A hairy and dusty smell, as if an old pet was cuddled up next to him. He could almost feel its fur in his hands.

Actually, he did. A thick, woolly pelt tickled his palms.

There were no pelts in the hab.

He sneezed.

Some dream.

"Floyd?" A woman's voice, gentle but insistent. "Floyd wake up. I gave you as long as possible, but I dozed off twice already, and that's no good."

"Huh?"

He sat and blinked.

"Wakey, wakey."

He was lying on a heap of furs, with more fur piled on top. A fire was roaring away, roasting his front with life-giving warmth.

His back wasn't quite so warm, but still okay.

Next to him sat Leela, yawning and stretching. It all came back to him. The strange woman who called herself El. The sea, the cave, the odd noises and lights in the sky.

If this was a dream, it was bloody realistic.

Shit.

"Sorry."

"It's fine. You weren't doing too well before we, eh...left, so it was logical to let you sleep. Do you feel better?"

Did he? Floyd listened to his heartbeat, a reassuringly steady rhythm in his chest. His head was doing okay as well, there was neither pressure, nor pain.

"I'll live. You go to sleep." Reluctantly, he rose from his warm nest and held a pelt out for her.

Leela nodded and settled herself on the furs. "Wake me if something happens."

"Sure."

As if he would. Her tawny face was gray with fatigue, her eyes bloodshot. She should have woken him a lot earlier, not when the pearly light of an early dawn was already lightening the shadows that lurked in their shelter.

She huddled in the pelts and closed her eyes. Only seconds later, her breath slowed and her face relaxed.

She was beautiful, really, with her high cheekbones and long lashes. Her hair was silky, made to cascade over her shoulders not be cut short to accommodate bloody space helmets.

If she could read his thoughts, she'd probably bop him one.

Floyd rose to check for firewood. There wasn't much left. If they stayed another night in this place they would have to—what was that?

Did he hear a noise coming from the crawl tunnel?

He strained his ears.

Nothing. He must have imagined things.

Crchh.

The faintest of noises reached his ears, a gentle brushing and a crunch so soft, it almost wasn't there. He tiptoed back to the fire and grabbed Leela's spear with one hand and a sturdy branch with another.

Armed stone-age style, he then crept to the entrance of the crawl tunnel.

The rustling had faded. In its stead white noise crackled in his ears, though that could also have been the fire. It was making a bloody racket—.

A hand appeared in the opening. Hairy, strong fingers with broad, flat nails grabbed the edge and held on.

Someone grunted, and there was a shuffling as if something heavy was trying to push through.

"Stop it right there." To emphasize his order, he banged the branch onto the floor.

The hand withdrew. The shuffling noises stopped.

Then, someone said something in a language he didn't understand. The voice was deep and calm, sounding questioning rather than menacing.

The owner of their shelter coming back from the hunt?

Someone's been sleeping in my bed and using up all the firewood.

"Sorry, mate." Floyd said. "We didn't have any choice. We've got some grilled fish left, if you like."

There was a response, but he didn't understand that either. The hand returned, waving at him.

He waggled the spear.

They had contact.

A second hand appeared, also waving and waggling its fingers. The hands seemed attached to hairy and worryingly brawny arms.

He took a step back, raising the spear in his hand.

With a groan, a huge slab of a man crawled from the hole and stood.

Shit. The guy was built like a brick outhouse with muscles that spoke of serious workouts. Fortunately, he also was old, the gray hair on his head thinning, his muscles corded strings in his arms. The guy's eyes were dark pools, shaded by a protruding brow ridge.

A male Neanderthal.

He was standing in a frigging cave with a male Neanderthal.

Oddly enough, the guy was smiling a rather gap-toothed smile. Dentists were probably making themselves scarce in this place. Not that it mattered. What mattered was the big, chunky rock of a guy examining him with a bemused expression on his bearded face.

The old Neanderthal pointed at the fire and moved his remaining chompers in a way that told Floyd he might be hungry. As if to ram the message home, he patted an ample belly protruding from the hides of assorted shaggy animals.

Floyd crab-stepped around him and pointed his spear at the fish Leela had lined up on a plank.

The Neanderthal man grunted, shuffled across, and sat down. It sounded like a minor earthquake.

It didn't take him long to plow his way through what was probably intended to be their breakfast. Oh well, if the guy was the owner of the shelter, they owed him.

When the old Neanderthal finally sucked his teeth, he sounded like a blender. Floyd winced, which got him an amused look. Then the guy said something.

"Sorry, I don't copy."

Oldie tapped his chest. "Mul."

He'd seen that movie.

"Ah. You Mul?" Floyd pointed at the man. "Me Floyd." He too tapped his chest. Since he still held the spear, he nearly cut off his nose.

"Floyeed?

"Yes, Floyd."

Mul grinned. Since there were bits of fish stuck in his teeth, it wasn't a pretty sight.

The heap of furs behind him moved, as Leela turned in her sleep.

Uh. What had he been thinking? What if Mul now got amorous?

But Mul was doing nothing of the sort. He peeped myopically around Floyd and raised his enormous brows in an unspoken question.

"Leela," Floyd said. He pointed at his chest. "Mine."

Urgh, he could only hope she didn't hear that. He'd never hear the end of it.

Mul only nodded, losing interest already.

Phew. Good job their visitor was an oldie. A young man might have been a different story.

A warm orange glare flooded the shelter with brightness. Sunrise.

That didn't work so well last time.

Mul rose and stretched, his enormous dark silhouette blocking the sun.

He then pointed at the opening of the shelter and said, "El."

Did he get that correctly? "El?"

Mul nodded and stepped aside.

He'd expected a Neanderthal woman wearing high-heels. Instead, he was facing an absolutely unbelievable sight. Floyd blinked.

From a sea of bluish mists rose a golden city.

Chapter 15

"Huh?" Floyd caught his jaw dropping, so he snapped it shut.

The city was still there. A living city, where lights now winked into being, and little dark shapes moved over an endless array of bridges, criss-crossing a void that must have been deeper than the Mariana Trench.

It sure looked that way—turquoise mists around the edges and a deepening blue below, as if a black hole had fallen into the ocean.

Muffled noises drifted across from afar, laughing and the shuffling of many feet. What looked like a caravan of people carrying packs on their backs was on the move, headed for the glittering maze of buildings.

"Huh," said Mul. It sounded satisfied, even slightly amused.

The big man stomped past the dying fire to the cave's ledge and waved at Floyd to follow. He swung around. Leela was still sleeping, her head on her smooth arms, a slight smile curving her lips.

Was she dreaming of protocols and life on Mars?

What's there to smile about?

"I can't leave her." Floyd pointed at the snoozing Mars mission commander. He bent over and picked up the last remaining log, which he then dumped onto the fire. Embers sparked and smoke puffed up.

Mul stomped back to Floyd's side and issued what sounded like a string of throaty consonants chasing each other's tails.

"Sorry?" Floyd asked.

On the bed of furs, Leela stretched, mumbled something, and turned her back on the fire.

Despite his apparent age, Mul crouched without effort, looking like a hairy boulder. He might have been rolling his eyes, but with the shadow thrown by his brow ridge, it was hard to tell what was going on in the wizened face underneath.

He pressed his hands together just like El had done.

Floyd tensed.

Uh, oh.

From between the old man's hairy paws rose a delicate tendril of opal smoke, gyrating like a translucent dancer. The smoke swirled and curled into a ball made of moving mists that threw a gentle glow on Mul's face.

The old man stood, opened his hands, and tossed the ball at the ceiling of the rock shelter. There it stuck, pulsating gently.

Mul then returned to the lip of the shelter, where the golden city still filled the view in Escher-like confusion. Bridges and stairs everywhere, crossing each other, leading to—that wasn't a city. That was a monstrous cliff dotted with glittery openings and slashed by horizontal ledges.

A bit like a super upmarket version of the Anasazi cliff dwellings laced with a hefty dose of surrealism. Some of the square structures slotted into the ledges looked like pastel-tainted Bauhaus mansions. Others bore rounded domes, like Greek churches in the Aegean sea. They weren't blue, though.

A seagull screeched past the shelter. So, presumably there was some sea around here somewhere.

A throaty hum filled the shelter, and it took Floyd a moment to suss that Mul was singing.

The seagull returned. This time, it shot straight into the cave.

At least, that must have been the intention. The bird rammed into an invisible obstacle and flumped to the floor.

There it sat, blinking in avine confusion.

Yeah, pal. You and me both.

Mul grinned. He pointed first at the bird, then at the ball.

"Is that a force shield?" Floyd asked. "How did you do that? We still can't make them happen."

Mul tilted his head. He tapped first his lips, then his head.

"You can't understand me? Well, we're in the same boat, then."

El had spoken his language. Odd that this guy couldn't when he could create force shields. With his hands. How cool was that?

An uncomfortable thought ignited in the recesses of Floyd's mind, took shape, and rose to the surface.

"Are you a magician or something? Shit, you still can't hear me."

Mul took a few measured steps and came to a stop. Up close, the guy really was enormous. But he didn't give off threatening vibes at all. Some of the serving crew in the canteen back at the training compound had been scarier, and they'd only been armed with ladles, not magic.

He also smelled…interesting. Of soil, mushrooms, and dried herbs with a bit of sweat mixed in, sure, but it wasn't old. And since Floyd had taken no shower yet, he doubted he'd be as fresh as lilies.

A cold blast buffeted Floyd, accompanied by a faint hissing and an even fainter klaxon screeching something about proximity alerts. Then it was gone.

"He's asking for permission to access your mind," a voice said behind him. It sounded snarky and no, it wasn't Leela's.

Slowly he swung around.

El was warming her hands at the fire, furs, heels at all. From her elbow dangled a small red handbag.

****

"Oh, now you show up," Floyd said.

"Would you like me to disappear again?"

"Not before you explained a few things. Like this." He pointed at the shelter. "And this." He pointed at the glowing city. "And while you're at it, you might introduce me to Mul. He's been a lot more polite than you. And keep your voice down. Leela needs her sleep."

El exposed her strong white teeth. "How sweet. I feel quite the matchmaker"

She swung around and sashayed over to where Mul stood, looking slightly perplexed.

That was interesting. It appeared the two Neanderthals didn't know each other. Fair enough, he didn't know every Tom, Dick, and Harry on this damned overpopulated Earth.

El let rip another endless string of consonants that crawled on top of each other until there was nothing but a verbal tangle.

Mul's response was just as knotted. He kept piercing the air with his index finger and his face flushed dark.

Someone wasn't happy.

El fished in her handbag and handed over something wrapped in a white paper. Mul hesitated, but then ripped off the paper and gulped down whatever she'd given him.

"Having problems?" Floyd asked.

"No," El said.

"Yes." Mul said, sucking on something which didn't help with his pronunciation.

"Ah," Floyd said. "Now it works."

El closed her handbag. "It's much easier to use potions than manipulate reality all the time. Less strain on the system."

Mul huffed and stood at the edge of the shelter. He spoke over his shoulder. "Just because you're from the future, it doesn't mean you're right. Looking at you gives me a pain in the butthole."

"You don't like my handbag?"

"Mammoth dung. I don't like you."

That made two of them. What did the guy just say?

"She's from the future?"

"Yes. So are you, correct?"

"I'm not sure we're from the same future."

"Of course not. You're a plainbrain. You're stuck in reality. Our people left for the Dream a long time ago. Well, seen from your perspective, they did it a long time ago. You witnessed the event last night. I guess that's why she sent you over here." Mul hooked a stubby thumb at a grinning El. "Not sure why, though."

"Because there was one teensie-weensie problem with us entering the Dream, Wiseman Mul."

"And that would be what, Wisewoman El?"

El pursed her mouth and spewed forth another incomprehensible hotchpotch of words.

"Oh," Mul said. "That's...not good."

For the first time, since Floyd had met the high-heeled Neanderthal woman, she looked worried.

"No, it isn't."

Chapter 16

Inside the cave, only the fire was moving. El, Mul, and Floyd stood rooted to the spot, silent. The orange flames spat out embers, billowed smoke, crackled and danced, their red sheen paling against the brightening sky and the sunlight reflecting from the cliff city. The cave walls reverberated with the happy echoes of laughter from the millipede made of people, still moving across bridges and up staircases, and then disappearing into the belly of the city.

Floyd cleared his throat. "You know, I've had it up to here with this mystery shit. Why don't you tell me what's going on, and I then decide what to do."

El pulled a wry smile. "That was my intention all along. Your skepticism doesn't make things easy."

"Of course, it's all my fault."

"I wasn't saying that at all. Tell me something. Do you believe in magic? I mean, do you do it now?"

Floyd stared first at the impossible city—were those glass panes? They couldn't be—and then at the high-heeled nuisance.

"Let's say I'm no longer ruling out the possibility that magic might exist."

El rolled her eyes. "You really are impossible."

"Hedging my bets, that's what I am."

Mul grunted something, and El flapped her hand. "Sure, sure. I was coming to the point."

"Good," said Floyd. "You can start with this." He pointed at the moving crowd where the last stragglers were hastening up the cliff face. "Are they leaving because it's so bloody cold?"

"No, they're leaving because of you."

"Me? Come on, that's unfair. I'm only here because of you."

El heaved a sigh. "Not you personally. Your people. What do you call yourselves? Homo sapiens? That's a good one. There's so much you don't know. Worse, you don't want to know. To compensate, you're as destructive as they come."

Floyd slammed through mental compartments in search of comebacks but found none. El wasn't wrong.

"Mh. So, what about this dream business? Is this something you created?"

For some odd reason, the comment drew hysterical laughter and much thigh-slapping from the two Neanderthals. Especially Mul had plenty of thigh to slap.

"Har, har. Very funny."

El wiped her streaming eyes. "I needed a good laugh."

"We can take and change what is there," Mul explained. "We cannot create what isn't there. We aren't gods."

"Just out of interest. Do they exist?"

Mul shrugged. "I do not know. I do not care. We have the dream, and we are content with it."

Floyd stared at the city.

"This was there. We changed it, so our people could come and live in it."

"Some sort of parallel reality?"

El wagged her head. "That probably describes it best, though Wiseman Mul here is perhaps being a bit simplistic. I'd say the potential for this"—she stabbed her finger in the air roughly where the city towered over the abyss—"existed. But we had to make it happen. Actually that's not quite right either. We are making it happen. All the time. It's the dream, you see?"

"Hah," said Mul.

Floyd didn't get it, not fully. "Mh. Complicated."

"Very. The dreams of our people ensure that what could be becomes and stays reality. Unfortunately, there's something else we need, and that we didn't know when we set out."

"Such as?"

"To use terminology you might understand, let me call it antimatter. We have positive energy from our people, but we also need the opposite to keep the dream stable. Unbelievers. People who can't dream. People who won't dream. People like you and her." El hooked her thumb at the still-sleeping Leela.

"Is this so?" Mul asked.

"Unfortunately, yes," El said. "We only noticed when the dream was fading and we lost quite a few of our people because of that. That was ten thousands of years ago. Fortunately, we only needed to, eh…boost our numbers with unbelievers once before."

"But why us? There are ten billion people on planet Earth you could chose from."

"You weren't on planet Earth. You were on Mars, remember?"

He did. Dimly.

"What has that got to do with the price of chips?"

"Mars is the gateway to the dream."

"Why?"

El massaged her temples. "See, this is why your species is such a nuisance. You keep asking questions all the time when some things simply are the way they are."

"We did not ask the red planet to be our gateway to the dream. We found out that this was the case, and we accepted it," Mul said.

Whoa. He had just mentioned planets. "You know about the sun, then? And the planets circling it?"

El and Mul looked at each other.

"They are such a nuisance, aren't they?" El said. "They seem to think all we ever did was hunt woolly mammoths, paint caves, grunt, and hit each other over the head with clubs."

As if to prove a point, Mul indeed grunted something.

"Well, we ensured we'd go extinct," El said. "So that one's correct at least. But otherwise? If we hadn't left some star charts and other useful stuff behind, you wise-asses would still squat in caves, believe me."

"Useful stuff?"

"Things like the wheel. How to tame wolves. That sort of thing."

"You're saying you sparked off civilization. Were there ever aliens? Are there any?"

"Here on Blueball?" Mul asked. "No. But they exist on other worlds. However, we only know of those we can speak to in the dream."

Floyd's head felt like it wanted to burst. This was all a bit much, so he latched on to the part that bothered him most.

"Do I understand correctly that you want us to join your dream? Leela and me?"

"Yes," El said. "Rest assured, I won't force you."

"Kind of you."

"Nah. It wouldn't work if I did. You need to make a conscious choice."

"Why would I do that? I mean, seriously, do you really expect us to join your world out of the kindness of our heart?"

El's smile was filled with teeth. "Of course not."

Oh?

"There's a catch, isn't there?"

The smile widened. "Isn't that always the case?"

"You could have asked Doc Bones. He's totally into that sort of stuff."

"You don't listen well," Mul said. "If we need unbelievers to maintain the balance, a believer won't do."

"He'll come along for the ride, though. I like him," El said.

Finally, they had something in common.

"Ah. Okay, makes sense in a weird way. What I don't get is this business with caves, writings on walls, bones hanging around—was that really necessary?"

"Would you have listened to me if I'd just showed up in your ugly habitation and told you what's what?"

"They are living on Redball?" Mul asked.

El wagged her head again. "Not really. They're trying but keep failing."

"Hey, we were peacefully setting things up, when you threw a spanner into the works. Not nice. You compromised the work of decades, you know?"

"Sorry for that. But the only ones who keep compromising things are you with your petty nationalism, and your never-ending aggressions. You're wasting so much energy on things that are dust only a few years later, it's painful to behold."

"Now you sound like one of these tree-huggers."

Mul nodded eagerly. "Tree-hugging is good. It yields more power for the dream."

"Not many trees left to hug, eh?" El said. "Anyway, we're getting distracted. More importantly, time is running out."

"For you?"

"No, for you."

Floyd's headache became more pronounced. His vision wobbled and then steadied again. Somewhere there was a shrieking noise, but that too went away.

"Let me see if I understand correctly. You want some non-magical people who don't believe in magic inside your magical construct, so it doesn't go kablowy on you."

"Correct."

"To achieve that, you come up with some weird stuff that has us running all over the place, scratching our heads over mobile caves, weird glyphs on the wall, and skeletons that are just as mobile as the cave."

"To soften you up, yes. It worked, didn't it? Created some lovely confusion. Confusion is creative. As is the dream. But you are truly hard-headed, so I had to show you this." In a sweeping gesture, she pointed at the walls of the cave. "Now, be honest. Do you believe in magic?"

Did he? Well in a way, he did. But this didn't make sense either.

"Hang on you just said you need unbelievers—"

"We do. Skeptics like you. But at the same time you have to be open to the concept. If your mind is totally closed, it won't work either. You're still doubting me. Which is good. But you're no longer blocking yourself."

"That doesn't mean we'll come with you." Leela stepped into the circle, an angry glitter in her eyes. "I overheard you, and I'm telling you, I'm not coming."

"Uh." If Floyd thought his head was about to burst earlier, he'd been quite wrong.

El's expression hardened. "We still have time to search for others. You're by no means my only choice. I simply thought it would make sense to offer you a chance."

"Very kind of you. But it's no thanks, and I'm sure Floyd here will agree," Leela said.

"Uh—" All this talk about grunting was getting to him.

"You shouldn't give me lip when you don't have all the facts," El said. "You might regret your decision. In fact, I'm sure you will." She glanced at a red smartwatch encircling her wrist. "In exactly two minutes and counting. Your time, of course, not ours."

Leela's expression segued to confused. "What are you on about?"

"I'm referring to the fact that your team never landed on Mars. That was all a dream I created for you. Your lander was flawed and you're about to shatter upon impact. Now, what do you say to my proposal?"

Chapter 17

The wail of a klaxon exploded into the cavern and bounced off the rocky walls. From nowhere, an acrid, eye-stinging mist drifted in, and the ground under Floyd's feet vibrated so hard, he stumbled toward the fire.

Only the fire wasn't there anymore.

In its stead an instrument panel rattled and shook into view, the source of the acrid fumes. Awash with a sea of blazing red lights, all of them flickering and flashing like lightning gone berserker, the panel took on substance until it completely blocked out the golden city.

Constant popping in Floyd's ears didn't quite muffle the shrill clamor of the klaxon. His body, encased in something a lot heavier and stiffer than furs, was being squashed into something soft, and there was a weight on his chest as if a mammoth was sitting on it.

"Floyd?" Someone screamed, sounding very much like Leela. But her voice was distorted and distant.

For a second, she sprung up in his peripheral vision, still clad in her furs, coughing and sputtering. Like a double image creeping in, a white garment materialized over her body, covering her legs, rump, and finally her arms. Where her head had been just a second ago, now sat a white, shiny bubble with a golden front.

His beleaguered brain, slow to throw out answers, seemed to believe she was wearing a spacesuit and a helmet.

The next instant, she was melting into some weird contraption his mind insisted on calling an APS, an Astronaut Protection Seat, the same thing he seemed to sit in.

"Leela," he screamed back.

The sound elongated into a screech, the shriek of tortured metal.

The cave, gone translucent like so much mist, lurched, sank, and bounced back up. Its walls disintegrated into something white, where cables swung as if shaken by a giant's fist.

"Now is a good time to make your choice." El's voice reflected the frozen nothingness between the stars.

Mul's response got swallowed into the din. His rugged features emerged from the chaos raging in the cave, concerned eyes staring from under the prominent brows. His lips were moving, but no sound came out. Or if it did, Floyd couldn't hear it. Then Mul became part of the haze that filled the cave, Floyd's mind, the solar system.

"Navigator DeNeville," Dr. Kalal yelled. "Manual override. Now."

Leela. She's called Leela.

"The parachutes!" Bones, seated on Floyd's other side, screamed.

There was no cave left.

Only a landing pod in serious trouble.

"Code Red. Hull breach. Code Red. Initialize emergency procedure. Code Red." That was the AI, steady, robotic, and supremely unconcerned about the mission's fate.

The mission. He was an astronaut, his job to prepare the colonization of Mars.

This meant...

Floyd opened his mouth, but no words came out. The weight on his chest was squeezing his ribs, clawing at his lungs.

It was hard, so hard, to turn his head toward the instrument panel. Red, red, wherever he looked. His gloved hands pawed at the controls. Altitude. It was all about altitude. Once he was in manual, there was no way back. If he engaged the parachutes too early, they would shred or burn. Or both. Whatever they did, the outcome would be the same.

The parachutes were vital.

As was SHIELD.

"Code Red. Hull breach." The damn AI warbling away in the background was as useful as heels on Mars.

The haze drifted, and for a heartbeat, the altimeter became visible. Too high. They were too bloody high.

"Can't...engage yet. A few kilometers We need...a few more kilometers."

The words were lost among the ringing in his ears, but he could swear the "shit" he might have heard had come from Bones.

Two minutes, El had said. This felt like a lifetime, but perhaps time itself had warped into eternity.

There is no El. There's only you.

He raised his gloved hand to wipe away the sweat on his forehead, but his visor was in the way.

Get a grip on yourself.

Floyd was a pro. He wasn't stressed. He mustn't be. Stressed astronauts soon turned into dead astronauts.

Something warm and wet trickled down his cheek. Astronauts didn't cry either. For no apparent reason, he thought of his mother.

Then he thought of Leela—Dr. Kalal.

Had he been dreaming while on duty and endangering the mission?

The haze in the cabin thinned.

That was bad news. It meant the smoke was getting sucked out through the hull breach. The rip or hole or whatever it was would be tiny, otherwise the damn...the blessed lander would have disintegrated into metal confetti a long time ago.

The turbulence eased off a bit.

Now, that was good news, which a quick scan of the altimeter confirmed. Close, they were getting so close. And wasn't that a green flare among all that red?

Fire-engine red. High-heel and handbag red.

Cut it out.

He squinted.

Yass!

The parachutes were still operational. As was the heat shield, another green glow right at the edge of the panel.

If they failed, they wouldn't be watching the show for very much longer.

Somewhere, there had to be two more green lights. Floyd's gaze jumped from one frantically blinking red light to the next—ah, there.

Double Yass!

SHIELD too was operational. They still stood a chance. No point in overriding anything for the moment. Let the auto-lander do the job.

But Floyd kept his finger hovering over the switch that would give him control.

One never knew.

El had fallen silent, but that didn't come as a big surprise. She'd never existed outside his mind. The whole crazy adventure had been a construct of his feverish brain.

Fever. Heat.

Rivulets of sweat ran down Floyd's back. The temperature in the lander reached toasty levels. Perhaps the heat shield was compromised, and that caused the hull breach?

Who cared? The fucking thing was doing enough to let them survive the atmospheric entry and deceleration phase.

Now they were trundling toward the surface.

The numbers on the altimeter changed to green.

"Going down," a disembodied voice said in Floyd's ear. It took a moment to match it with Bones, seated on his left.

Let the parachutes function. Please let them function. And don't forget SHIELD.

Its accordion-like, collapsible base acted like the crumple zone of a car and absorbed the energy of a hard impact. Much better than using only parachutes in Mars's thin atmosphere. That was really dangerous, and that's how the first teams of pre-colonists were lost.

They mustn't be lost. They still had a chance to land and write history.

If he stopped talking to himself.

"Activating parachutes," the AI said in what sounded like an unnecessarily cheerful voice.

The landing pod jerked and swung aside like an over-sized gong. For a moment, it hung suspended in midair before it continued the descent, only much slower.

The parachutes were working. Floyd sent a silent prayer to some forever unknown technicians who bolted the blessed pod together—

From Floyd's left came an ominous crunching noise.

He held his breath.

Nothing happened.

"Yes! We're gonna make it." That had been Dr. Kalal. She really should know better than to say such things before they were down.

"Shut your gob," Bones said.

My sentiments entirely.

"Hull breach. Code Red," said the AI. It had probably been repeating the message on an auto-loop. Or perhaps not.

Did it matter? Hardly.

"Tell me something I don't know," Floyd said. Oddly enough, talking had become easier. While his chest still ached and burned, at least the pressure had eased.

Surely, the two minutes had been passed a while ago.

Forget about this countdown rubbish. Forget about El. She never existed. Do your job.

His job was to land the mission safely. His job was to get them down in one piece. With a pierced hull, and the heavens only knew how many systems damaged. But if the inflatable heat shield and the deflector had sort of worked, and if the parachutes continued to do their job, perhaps SHIELD, the most important system of them all would also function.

"Code Red," said the AI and died on a burp.

Well, that wasn't a big loss.

"Proximity alert," another recorded voice said, as calmly as if it was commenting on a town parade.

Bullshit. We're not at the surface yet. Bloody Yackety-yack all the time.

"Prepare yourselves," Floyd said. "Landing's gonna be rough."

"Yeah," said Bones.

"Stop talking and do your job," said Leela. "Uh, sorry. I didn't mean it like that."

He seriously had no time for this bullshit.

Floyd turned down the transmission to a whisper. If anyone wanted something from him, they could use the override button. Then he checked his harness. It seemed to sit where it was supposed to be sitting.

Something rumpled, and the pod wobbled. Floyd's stomach lurched, but settled again when the pod steadied.

He placed his hand on the vibrating instrument board, close to the controls. How he itched to grab them, but intervention and mission override were only for dire emergencies. Which this wasn't, not yet, no matter what the blasted AI thought. The hull might be breached, but it wasn't disintegrating; they were out of the thermal zone. The longer the pod continued in autopilot mode, the better. But he'd intervene if he had to—

Scrunch.

It was such a tiny noise, really.

One side of the lander peeled off. Just like that.

Where the wall on Floyd's left had been, there suddenly was a boiling, howling orange tempest.

The next instant, Bones was gone, sucked into the maw of the raging wind that yanked the pod around as if it were wadded tissue.

"Noooo."

The scream wasn't his.

And then it was gone.

Where there had been turbulence before, there now was madness. Up was down and down was up. Every bone in Floyd's body was squeezed by a giant fist that pressed the air from his lungs. His teeth hurt, his brain was pounded into a mash, and a hurricane was ripping at the wrecked lander. To his right, something white flailed about.

Leela was still there.

"Evac imminent!"

Floyd slammed his fist on the big orange switch, the only one that hadn't been flickering.

With a thunderous roar, a square part of the lander blew off and Floyd's APS launched from the doomed pod.

Leela shot past him, her seat framed in a halo of booster fire.

She stretched out her hands, as if reaching out, and he caught himself doing the same. Their gloved hands brushed past each other, accompanied by the fiendish roaring of the orange wind.

But he could swear he heard a whisper over the comms unit.

"I love you. Always did. That's why..."

She arched out of sight, yanked up by her parachutes.

She might yet make it. Might be safe.

But in his heart, he knew the truth.

The whisper was sucked into the scream of the tempest raging around Floyd.

A jerk shuddered through his body as his parachute engaged.

He still was way too fast. There was no need to check any measurements. He knew it in every doomed bone.

The seat had no SHIELD. The seat would crash and smear his body all over Mars's surface. His and Leela's.

Bones at least would have been dead immediately.

Small blessing.

Tears running down his cheeks, Floyd cavorted through the heavens until the heavens parted, and there was ground beneath him, rushing up fast as if eager to greet him.

If only there was magic.

If only the dream was real.

But all he had was science, broken like his bones would soon be.

"Save Leela. Do you hear?" he screamed at the void. "If you can't save me, save her."

The void took on a golden sheen, and he could swear he heard the shriek of a seagull.

Then the void reached up and sucked him in.

Epilogue

Silence hung over Mission Control. One by one, headphones were torn from anguished ears and computers switched off. One after the other, the controllers shambled from the room, leaving only one station occupied.

One after the other, the lights went out. Microphones ceased their incessant blare.

The mission had been a failure; the three astronauts lost.

There wouldn't be another mission, at least not in the near future.

Sightlessly, Dr. Paulson stared at the screen where the robot camera on PEMAR had been recording the disaster once the in-lander transmission failed.

The landing pod disintegrating, an enormous chunk torn from its side.

A white-suited figure shooting out, spiraling downward and vanishing into the mists that flowed around the rocks in a milky spill.

Then a soundless explosion as the navigator did his job and initiated ejection. Two seats launching into the sky, two parachutes opening, two figures hurtling down.

If they'd been a hundred meters or so farther up, they might have made it.

But the planet's thin atmosphere granted no mercy.

Much too fast, the two figures rushed to their fate, sending up curried clouds of dust as they slammed into the ground.

A controller had remote-driven PEMAR across. Mission-control owed them that much. They'd found all three bodies. Oddly enough, they'd been lying within meters of each other, the parachutes draped over the broken remains like plastic shrouds.

It was better that way.

PEMAR was now back at the base, awaiting a crew that might never come.

With a sigh, Dr. Paulsen rose and shuffled after his colleagues.

The Mars winds billowed icy gusts into the shrouds, flapping and fluttering like restless specters trying to escape Fate.

Then the air shimmered. A brownish smear took on the shape of a woman wearing twinkly layers of furry hides, beads and feathers dangling from every possible and impossible part of her clothing.

She wore red high heels and carried a handbag of the same color.

"That was quite unnecessary, you know?" she addressed the shredded parachutes and their grisly cargo hidden within.

"You doubted again, both of you. I read it in your minds. Bones is fine. He believed in me from the start. He's already dreaming."

El sighed. "What am I to do with you two? Well, I guess, you both sort of came around right at the end. That was actually quite touching, the way you wanted me to save each other. And you both used the m-word. And the d-word. There's nothing like a good romance, told by the fireside, eh? I guess, I'll let it stand. Today's your lucky day. Welcome to the dream."

She smiled once more and then faded. Where she had stood, dust and grit dropped away, forming a vast crater that swallowed the bodies of the three astronauts and the parachutes covering them.

When the dust flowed back, not a trace remained on the surface.

Under the surface, cradled in the sand, a skeleton materialized next to the bodies. A seagull shrieked once.

Then darkness.